DR. DOLITTLE 2

YEARLING BOOKS are designed especially to entertain and enlighten young people. Patricia Reilly Giff, consultant to this series, received her bachelor's degree from Marymount College and a master's degree in history from St. John's University. She holds a Professional Diploma in Reading and a Doctorate of Humane Letters from Hofstra University. She was a teacher and reading consultant for many years, and is the author of numerous books for young readers.

DR. DOLITTLE 2

**Based upon the Doctor Dolittle Stories by
HUGH LOFTING**

**Based upon the motion picture written by
LARRY LEVIN**

**Novelization by
LARA BERGEN**

A Yearling Book

35 Years of Exceptional Reading

Yearling Books
Established 1966

Published by
Dell Yearling
an imprint of
Random House Children's Books
a division of Random House, Inc.
1540 Broadway
New York, New York 10036

Visit us on the Web! www.randomhouse.com/kids

Educators and librarians, for a variety of teaching tools, visit us at www.randomhouse.com/teachers

ISBN: 0-440-41828-3

Printed in the United States of America
May 2001
10 9 8 7 6 5 4 3 2 1
OPM

Chapter 1

Dr. Dolittle was busier than ever. At ten he had
Mr. Carson coming in for a full checkup. At twelve he
had Mr. Wennington scheduled for an EKG. And in
between he had to squeeze in Mrs. Bloom and her
itchy rash.

But that wasn't all. At twelve-thirty Buster was
due for his worming. At one Misty was having her
kennel cough looked at. And the rest of the afternoon . . . well, that was wall-to-wall neuterings.

Then there was the Rotary Club dinner that night,
and the Kennel Club breakfast the next morning.

It was truly as much as Dr. Dolittle, his secretary,
and his shaggy canine assistant, Lucky, could handle.

Ever since the doctor had discovered he could talk
to animals—and understand what they were saying—

he had devoted his life to helping them as well as helping people. He traveled all over the world rescuing animals in need. He led support groups for strays at neighborhood shelters. He settled feuds and lovers' quarrels at the most prestigious zoos. And naturally he made the rounds of all the nature shows: *National Geographic Explorer, Emergency Vet, Crocodile Hunter*—you name it, he was there.

In fact, Dr. Dolittle was becoming quite a celebrity. He couldn't even go home without being swarmed by furry and feathered groupies.

"There he is! It's him!" they screeched one night as he drove up to his apartment.

"He's so handsome! Sign my food dish!" they howled. "Touch my paw!"

With a modest nod, the doctor pushed past them toward his door.

"Thank you," he replied. "Thank you all very much!" He fumbled for his keys.

"Not again." He sighed as he searched his empty pockets. Brushing pet hair from his suit, he pressed a buzzer on the wall.

"Who is it?" a canine voice coyly barked from his apartment.

"It's me, Lucky," said Dr. Dolittle. "I forgot my keys."

"Well, then I guess you'll have to beg," the mutt inside teased.

Dr. Dolittle grumbled and leaned on the buzzer once again.

"Come on, boy, beg," Lucky went on. "Get it? Role reversal . . . 'Cause usually the human says to the dog . . . uh . . ."

"Lucky!"

"Oh, all right."

Lucky pressed a button with his paw and the outside door buzzed open.

Seconds later, an exhausted Dr. Dolittle walked into his apartment.

"Hey, sweetie," called his wife, Lisa. She worked long hours as an attorney but almost always made it home before the doctor did.

"Hey, baby." Dolittle smiled and kissed her warmly on the lips. Then he reached into his pocket and pulled out a gift-wrapped box. "A little present for you. From Paris."

Lisa dutifully took it and placed it on a table piled high with other tokens he had given her. Dolittle always brought his family gifts from the faraway places he visited.

"Thank you," she told him. "But you know what would be a nice present, John?" She nodded wearily toward the window. "Keeping your flock of the faithful away from our building."

Dolittle nodded. He loved helping animals, but sometimes the constant pressure was a bit much. He kissed his wife again. "I'll go down and talk to them later."

Suddenly his youngest daughter, Maya, dashed in.

"Daddy!" she yelled as she wrapped her arms around him.

"Hey, sweet girl!" He hugged her back. Then he pulled out another brightly wrapped present and gave it to her. "From Mexico."

"*Gracias,*" said Maya with a grin. "I wonder what it is."

She held it up to her ear and gave it a little shake.

"Aaaah! Earthquake!"

Dolittle's ears pricked at the sound of the voice hollering inside the box. He could understand the accented voice, but Maya could not.

"Eet's the big one!" the tiny voice cried.

"Er, honey," Dr. Dolittle warned his daughter, "I wouldn't do that."

Obediently Maya set down the box and opened it carefully. Inside she found a rattled-looking bright green lizard.

"Oh, he's so cute!" Maya exclaimed. "Thanks, Dad!"

"It's a chameleon," Dolittle told her. "His name is Pepito. He can change colors to blend into the background. Watch." Gently he picked Pepito up by his tail and placed him on the brown dining room table.

The lizard stood proudly at attention. "Now you see me . . . ," he announced, ". . . *poof!*" He squeezed his eyes shut. "Now you don't!"

Dr. Dolittle and Maya stared at the green creature and waited a moment. But he still stood out just as much as he had before.

"Um, we still see you," Dolittle whispered.

Just then Lisa walked up behind them. "You did remember it's Charisse's birthday?" she asked, cocking a wary eyebrow at him.

"Of course!" Dolittle nodded. Birthdays were always a big deal in the Dolittle household. "Did you get the cake from Stinson's?"

"Hey, *ese.*" The little chameleon called out to him from below, still trying to camouflage himself. "How about now? Gone, right?"

Dolittle glanced down at the pesky creature, who was still bright green.

"No," he said. He turned back to his wife, who was shaking her head.

"Charisse doesn't want a family birthday party," she told him.

Dolittle frowned. "Nonsense! We always celebrate as a family."

"It's this table," Pepito meanwhile muttered. "I

have trouble with brown. Do you have anything green?"

"She's got a date," Lisa went on, oblivious to the chameleon.

"A date?" Dolittle's frown deepened. "With who?"

"I didn't ask," his wife replied. "She's a big girl now, John."

"A date? Humph. We'll see about that."

By now Dr. Dolittle had forgotten about the plight of the Mexican guest on his dining room table.

"You know, something nice and green, like a head of lettuce," Pepito was saying. "Or some guacamole."

Dolittle rolled his eyes and turned to Maya. "Could you take him to your room, please?" he groaned with a wave toward the chameleon.

"You're so adorable," Maya crooned, cradling the chameleon in her palms as she hurried off. "I think I'm going to love you!"

The doctor took a step toward Lisa. "Now where's the birthday girl?"

"She's unreachable," his wife replied.

"Unreachable where?"

"She's in her room with the door locked and head-phones on." Lisa shrugged. "You could try paging her."

"Paging her!" Dolittle exclaimed. "In my own house?" He turned and stomped off toward his older daughter's room. "I don't think so."

Faithfully the mutt Lucky followed him to Charisse's door.

"Charisse. Charisse!" Dolittle hollered as he knocked.

"Try her cell," the dog suggested.

The doctor shook his head and banged on the door once more, disgusted. "Call my own daughter in my own home on a cell phone? Ridiculous!"

Glaring, he glanced at the hall window, stepped up to it, and slid it open.

Chapter 2

Moments later, fifty feet above the cold, hard ground, Dr. Dolittle inched his way along the fire escape toward Charisse's bedroom window.

Suddenly, a furry gray face dropped down in front of him.

"I have a message from the beaver," a wiry possum declared, swinging by his thin pink tail.

The doctor stared at him, confused. "The who?"

"The beaver. He needs to see you. It's life or death."

Dolittle frowned at the creature and impatiently brushed past him. "Tell whoever that is he's got to make an appointment. Just like everybody else."

"I can't tell him that," the possum squeaked. "I'll wind up part of a dam somewhere."

But Dolittle wasn't listening. He was too busy trying to get his teenage daughter's attention. He knocked on her window and shouted her name. But with her headphones on and her brown eyes glued to her dancing reflection in the mirror, she heard and saw nothing. It was useless.

Dolittle braced himself on the fire escape and gave the window a shove—only to find it was locked tight as a drum. He banged on the glass once more. Then finally, to his great chagrin, he gave up, pulled his cell phone from his pocket, and began to dial.

"Yeah?" Charisse cheerfully answered as she flipped open her own phone. "Daddy? Is that you? Slow down. I can't understand you. Where are you calling from? Daddy!"

Wide-eyed, Charisse spun around to see her dad's face pressed against her window.

"Daddy!" she cried as she raced over and let him in. "When did you get home?"

"What's this about not wanting to celebrate your birthday with your family?" Dolittle snapped, getting right to the point.

"Dad." Charisse groaned. "Having dinner with your family on your birthday is what you do when you're little. Not when you're sixteen. Besides, I have a date."

"You can invite your date," Dolittle told her generously.

Charisse rolled her eyes. "Oh, cool. So I'll say, 'Eric, these are my parents and my little sister, they'll be joining us on our date.' *Please!*"

"No," Dolittle corrected her. "He's joining *us*. This is a family event. We always— What's this?"

Dolittle's eyes drifted down to a sheet of paper on Charisse's bed.

"Hey, that's private!" Charisse shouted, lunging for the sheet.

But her father beat her to it.

"Your report card . . . Three Cs and a D?" he exclaimed. "These grades are embarrassing!"

"Embarrassing?" Charisse scoffed. "Daddy, you're the last person who should be talking about anything being embarrassing."

Dolittle frowned. "What does that mean?" he asked, somewhat hurt.

Charisse nodded toward the window and the possum still dangling from the fire-escape railing.

"Okay." Dolittle sighed. "So what do you think I should do? Give up my work . . . stop helping animals because it embarrasses you?"

Charisse looked down and shuffled her feet. "That's not going to happen," she grumbled.

"You're right," Dr. Dolittle replied. "So you'll just have to learn how to deal with it." Clicking his tongue, he neatly folded her heinous report card, then reached out and took her phone. "Get ready for dinner," he said matter-of-factly. "No cell phone for a week."

Charisse's mouth fell open. "Daddy!" she cried. "What am I supposed to do without a cell phone?"

Dolittle took out his wallet and produced a postage stamp. "Write a letter," he said, smiling.

"Teenagers!" Dr. Dolittle groaned as he walked out of Charisse's room.

Boy, how things had changed. What ever happened to that sweet little girl he used to know? The one who got good grades and liked to do things with her family—and who thought he hung the moon.

Recently he felt as if he had nothing in common with Charisse. But at least, he told himself, he could still relate to his baby, Maya . . . for now.

Dolittle's thoughts were interrupted when he rounded a corner and saw a very serious-looking bobcat staring in at him from the patio.

Dolittle sighed and looked down at the mutt still following close at his heels. "Lucky, can you deal with this, please?"

"Sure thing, Doc," Lucky panted. And as Dr. Dolittle walked on to the kitchen, the dog nudged the French doors open and stepped outside onto the patio.

"What's up?" he asked the cat.

"I gotta see the doc," the bobcat answered stiffly.

"Not a chance," Lucky told him with a flick of his tail. "Doc sees predators on Tuesdays."

"It's not for me," the big cat explained. "I got a message from the beaver."

Lucky shrugged. "Come back Tuesday."

"I can't take that back to the beaver!" the bobcat growled. "I could eat you, you know."

"Yeah, yeah." Lucky scratched his ear and turned around. "Tuesday."

Meanwhile, back inside, Dolittle was playing with Charisse's cell phone. "This is unbelievable," he said, shaking his head. "Charisse has fifty phone numbers in memory. And not one of them is mine."

"You shouldn't be looking at that," Lisa said, fastening a button on her shirt.

He read through the names his daughter had penned in. "Biggie Mack, cell. Biggie Mack, home. Biggie Mack, pager. Who's Biggie Mack?"

Lisa shrugged.

Dolittle punched in the number.

"What are you doing?" Lisa asked, frowning. "John!"

Dr. Dolittle listened. A voice answered. "Hello?" Little did Dr. Dolittle know that the voice belonged to Biggie Mack's father, Eldon.

"Who's this?" barked Dolittle.

"Who's this?" Eldon asked, annoyed.

"Is this Biggie Mack?"

Obviously Eldon had no idea, but he wasn't going to admit that. "Who wants to know?"

"How old are you?" demanded Dolittle.

"None of your business!" Eldon hollered.

Dolittle could feel his face getting hot. "Well, I'm going to *make* it my business."

"You threatening me?" Eldon shouted.

"You want to come and find out?" Dolittle egged him on.

"John!" Lisa grabbed the phone. "I'm sorry, wrong number," she apologized into the receiver before clicking off.

"That was a grown man I was talking to," Dolittle burst out, pacing the floor.

"Can't say the same about you," Lisa said, shaking her head. "Did it ever occur to you that Biggie Mack might have an overprotective father just like you? Honestly."

At that moment the doorbell chimed through the Dolittle apartment.

"I'll get it," Dolittle called, trying to calm down. He made his way to the front door and pulled it open.

"Doctor D!" exclaimed a tall, dark-skinned boy in baggy pants and a down jacket.

"I'm sorry . . . ," Dolittle began, bewildered. Did he know this young man? Could this be Biggie Mack?

"Domino's pizza, extra cheese, extra anchovies. I delivered it!" The teenager grinned a friendly, toothy grin. "You're the bomb, man," he went on, reaching for the doctor's hand. "Gettin' jiggy with the piggies."

Doctor Dolittle shrank back from the kid's elaborate handshake. "Did I not tip you?" he asked nervously.

The boy's eyes twinkled. "You gave me something much better than a tip," he said with a wink.

"Hi, Eric!"

Dolittle spun around to see Charisse, dressed in a new outfit and wearing a fresh layer of makeup, eagerly walking toward them. And suddenly it hit him.

"*This* is your date?" he exclaimed.

Charisse grinned and nodded. "Dad, Eric. Eric, Dad. Bye, Dad." Then she casually breezed past him.

"You sure you won't stay?" he asked with a hopeful pout.

Charisse flashed him a "yeah, right" look out of the corner of her eye.

"Mean a lot to me," he said. And with that he pulled out her cell phone and waved it in front of her eyes.

Charisse sighed and bit her lip. Then, reluctantly, she grabbed the phone.

"Okay," she muttered, "but after the cake, we're

outta here." Flipping her hair, she headed for the dining room.

"Don't worry," Eric said as he and Dolittle watched her go. "I know how to handle her."

And with another knowing wink, he strutted off in Charisse's direction.

That, thought Dolittle with a sinking feeling in his stomach, *is exactly what I'm scared of!*

Chapter 3

By the time the main course of the birthday dinner was on the table, Dr. Dolittle was really on a roll. And Charisse was sorrier than ever that she'd agreed to stay at all.

"Charisse always had a mind of her own," the doctor said fondly, beaming as he dished out the lasagna. "She couldn't have been more than a year and a half when she refused to wear diapers anymore—"

"John—" Lisa cut in.

But Dr. Dolittle laughed and went on. "Of course, then she started having all these little accidents around the house, so we had to paper train her."

"Daddy!" Charisse cried. Frantically she motioned toward Eric with her eyes.

"No," Eric said, chuckling along with Dolittle and Maya. "I don't mind. I'm learning a lot."

Lisa tried to save her daughter by changing the subject. "Sixteen!" she exclaimed. "Charisse, in two years you'll be out of the house and off to college."

"One year, ten months, sixteen days," Charisse corrected huffily.

"Berkeley's a good school," Dolittle reminded her. "You could stay in San Francisco. Live at home. Save some money."

"Daddy," Charisse informed him, "I've already reserved a U-Haul for the day I graduate high school."

Before Dolittle could reply, a tap on the window made everyone turn around.

"Dad! Someone else to see you," announced Maya, pointing at the window with her fork.

Staring in at them through his dark fur mask was an irate and rather overweight raccoon.

The doctor served up the last plate, then pushed his chair back from the table.

"I'll be right back," he told his family.

Outside on the balcony, Dolittle sourly faced his visitor.

"What is it?" he grumbled.

"First," began the raccoon, "let me say the beaver sends birthday greetings to your lovely daughter."

"Oh, that's very nice," Dolittle said, rolling his

eyes. "Now, you tell this beaver he's starting to get on my nerves." And with that he turned to go back inside.

"He wishes only a moment of your time," the raccoon said quickly.

Dolittle stopped. "And if I say no?"

The raccoon twitched his whiskers. "I don't think that's an option."

"Fine." The doctor sighed. "Tell him I'll see him tomorrow—eight o'clock at my office."

But the raccoon shook his head. "The beaver doesn't travel," he said. Then he leaned in closer to the doctor. "He knows you are a busy man. He will remember this. . . . It truly is a life-or-death situation."

Dr. Dolittle considered his words for a moment. "Okay," he said finally. "Seven A.M. My car."

"This is good news," the raccoon said, rubbing his paws together. "The beaver likes good news."

Just then a hand knocked on the window. It was Lisa signaling that it was time for Charisse's birthday cake.

"Go," said the raccoon with a grateful nod. "Enjoy."

Both annoyed and puzzled by the raccoon's demands, Dolittle stepped back into the dining room. At the head of the table, Charisse was just about to blow out her birthday candles.

"Make a wish," Lisa reminded her with a smile.

Charisse stared down at her sixteen candles, then up at her father. Then she closed her eyes, took a deep breath, and—

"Surprise!"

"Happy birthday!"

Out of the cake popped two icing-faced, crumb-covered rats.

"Ahhhh!" shrieked Charisse, jumping back. *"Daddy!"* she cried, pointing to the rodents, who were fighting over one of the birthday candles.

"John!" Lisa echoed. Maya hid behind her.

"This wasn't *my* idea!" Dolittle assured them.

With a stern glare, he scooped the rats up by the scruffs of their necks and carried them outside to the balcony.

"We just wanted to do something nice for your daughter," the first rat tried to explain, his tiny rodent feet sticky with frosting.

"Yeah," added the other. "If a little kitty had popped out, everybody'd be goin' *'Ohhh!'*"

"You're not little kitties," Dolittle growled. "You're filthy, disgusting rats!"

"Sticks and stones," declared the first rat. "You know what *rats* spells backwards? *Star!*"

"Yeah." The second rat nodded. "I'm a star!"

"I'm a star too," said the first.

"You know what *ha* spells backwards?" Dolittle

asked them as he stretched his arms out over the balcony, dangling them by their tails. Then with a tight grin, he let the rats go.

"*Ahhhhhh!*" they wailed as they fell like two sticky pink snowballs into the Dumpster below.

Dolittle wiped his hands. "Exactly," he said.

Later that evening, after Charisse and Eric had gone out, Dolittle tried his best to get back on his wife's good side.

"You know I had nothing to do with that rat thing," he told her, adjusting his bathrobe.

"John." Lisa sighed. "That's always your excuse. You can't control the animals, but you've got to admit you haven't exactly discouraged them either."

"What does that mean?" asked Dolittle, flushing.

"It means that some of this has gone to your head, John."

He tried to look shocked. "You think I *like* all this?"

"Yes." Lisa nodded. She stopped brushing her hair and folded her arms across her chest. "It's completely understandable." She shrugged. "Who doesn't want to feel needed . . . or in your case, worshipped? Just know that we're suffering the consequences."

She stared hard at Dolittle and waited for him to respond. But the doctor didn't know what to say.

He'd never asked for all this attention. She knew that. And besides, he asked himself, why should he have to explain himself to her or Charisse or anyone else? He was just using his gift—and doing his job. *Helping* people . . . or animals, he should say.

Then again . . . maybe she was right. Maybe his occupation *was* taking over all their lives. . . .

He didn't know, and he didn't think he was up to figuring it out that night. It was late. He was tired. So without replying, he simply turned and walked away.

Meanwhile, in Charisse and Maya's room, another Dolittle was trying her best to hone the family skill.

"What are you doing?" Charisse asked when she came home from her birthday date.

Maya's eyes were glued to Lucky's and her forehead was wrinkled in intense concentration. "I think he's about to say something," she said out of the corner of her mouth.

In fact, the dog was trying his best to tell Maya, "Bring me a bone." But unfortunately Maya hadn't picked up on it yet.

"Is it, like, your dream to become a freak?" her older sister asked, dismayed.

Maya frowned. "*Daddy* isn't a freak," she replied.

"No?" said a dubious Charisse.

"He's a great, famous man," declared Maya, "and I'm going to learn to talk to animals and be just like him and you'll be crying, 'Boo-hoo, she can do it and I can't.'"

Charisse rolled her eyes. "Yeah, right."

Maya shrugged away her sister's sarcasm and focused once again on Lucky. "Come on, Lucky, talk to me, boy."

"You will bring me ham," the dog pleaded—though apparently to no avail.

At last Charisse had had enough. "Lucky, out!" she called, swinging the bedroom door wide open.

Obediently Lucky stood up and exited the room—but not before trying one last time to talk to Maya.

"Luncheon meats . . . ," he whined. "Cold cuts."

"Out!" Charisse repeated.

"Oh, well," sighed Lucky. He trotted down the hall just as Dr. Dolittle stepped into view.

"Hey, girls," the doctor called warmly.

Charisse looked away. "Hi," she mumbled.

"I'm sorry about tonight," he said, resting in the doorway. "I'm going to try to cut back a little bit. Spend some more time here with you guys."

Charisse glanced at him out of the corner of her eye. "Then more animals would be around *here*," she said dryly.

"Well, I was thinking about taking the whole family to Europe this summer. . . ."

Charisse spun around. "Seriously?" She gasped.

"Yeah." Dolittle grinned and nodded. "Paris, Rome, the Greek islands. We've always talked about it. Let's do it."

Charisse's eyes narrowed. "Are you trying to bribe me again?"

Her father winked. "Yeah."

"It's working." Charisse laughed.

But before they could get any further in their plans, an eager rap sounded at the window.

Dr. Dolittle glared over Charisse's shoulder at the raccoon on the sill. "I said tomorrow!" he snapped.

"What?" asked Charisse, confused.

"I . . ." Dolittle looked down at her guiltily and gulped. "I'll call the travel agent tomorrow," he promised.

Chapter 4

Before any vacation plans were made, however, Dr. Dolittle had a bit of business to attend to. So first thing the next morning, he met the possum and the raccoon and drove out to the beaver's forest.

"Nice ride," said the raccoon, settling back in his seat as they headed over the Golden Gate Bridge. "What do you call this?"

"A Mustang," said Dolittle, his eyes focused on the heavy traffic.

"Is there a car named after me?" the possum inquired.

"A Possum?" Dolittle looked doubtful. "I don't think so."

The possum sighed. "Pity."

On the other side of the bridge, the raccoon

directed Dolittle into a lush green forest and out onto a remote fire road. They drove beneath a canopy of giant cedars until they reached a slow, winding stream. That was when the raccoon motioned for Dolittle to stop.

"This way," he told the doctor.

Obediently Dolittle got out of the car and followed the raccoon and possum down a mossy path.

"It's him! It's Dr. Dolittle!" the birds above them chirped.

"Everything's going to be okay!"

"I figured he'd be taller. . . ."

At last the group found itself in a clearing where the stream flowed into a tranquil pond.

"Nice spot," admitted Dolittle as he looked around, admiring the scenery. "But where's—"

"Over here," called a deep voice.

Dr. Dolittle turned to see a large, distinguished-looking beaver sitting on a thronelike rock and chewing on a stick. Around him were gathered several other forest creatures: some squirrels and rabbits, several woodchucks, a wolf, a few deer, and the bobcat from the night before.

"What took you so long?" asked the bobcat.

The beaver flashed him a warning look. "That's enough!" he scolded. "I'm sorry," he told Dolittle. "He's a hothead. Would you like a fish?"

He waved his stick at a pile of trout sitting by his

rock. From their blank eyes and strong odor, Dolittle could tell they were dead.

"Uh, no thank you," he said.

"The beaver offers you a fish," the raccoon snapped, waddling up behind him, "you take a fish!"

"Joey!" the beaver called, slapping his tail. He shook his head and motioned for the raccoon to take a seat. Then he turned back to his guest of honor.

"Thank you for coming," he told Dolittle calmly. "I've heard good things about you. From some of the Bay Area families."

"What is this," Dolittle asked, half-joking, "like, the Mafia?"

"Mafia?" yelped the raccoon. "We don't know nothin' about any Mafia, do we, boys?"

The other animals shook their heads wildly.

"No."

"Nope."

"Never heard of it," they swore.

The beaver looked down and smoothed his fur. "I'm just a simple fisherman who's blessed with many friends," he modestly explained. "Perhaps you will be one of them."

"Okay," Dolittle said after a moment's hesitation. "So what do you want from me?"

"I'm losing my territory," the beaver said.

"Some other animal moving in?" asked Dolittle.

"Yeah," the beaver replied coldly. "The human kind.

They're cutting down our homes. Busting up families. Word is, they're taking down the whole forest."

"You've gotta make them stop," the possum pleaded.

"Oh, now . . ." Dolittle held up his hands and shook his head. "You need to talk to one of those tree-hugging groups. Sierra Club or—"

"It has to be *you*, Doc," the beaver told him. "You're the only one we know who speaks human."

"Yeah," said the raccoon. "We can't fight humans on our own. They've got guns and machines and those Swiss Army knives with corkscrews and tooth-picks and teeny tiny scissors."

"We can't compete with that!" the possum exclaimed.

"Listen," said the doctor, "I wish I could help, but it's not that simple. There's something called the U.S. Forest Service, and they've got rules and regulations—" He gazed around at the sad, puzzled expressions on the desperate creatures' faces. "And you have no idea what I'm talking about, do you?"

"Sure I do," said the beaver. "It's man against nature. But with you on our side"—he grinned through his long, yellow teeth—"I like our odds."

And with that the beaver climbed down from his rock and began to waddle away.

"Wait, wait," Dolittle called after him. "I didn't say I was going to help you."

But the beaver didn't seem to hear.

Within moments the other animals followed him, leaving Dolittle alone in the peaceful clearing.

He groaned at the mess he had somehow gotten himself into. But he wasn't going to stay in it. No way were a bunch of animals going to bully him into something he didn't want to do—and didn't have the *power* to do. No way!

Grumpily he made his way back to the road where his car was parked and climbed inside. If he hurried, he thought as he drove back toward the highway, he could still be in his office in time for his ten o'clock appointments and have his family's vacation plans made by the afternoon. . . .

Suddenly he stopped the Mustang.

Slowly Dr. Dolittle opened the door, got out, and walked to a ridge by the side of the road. What he saw laid out before him on the other side made him gasp. In stark contrast to the emerald forest he'd been driving through, the valley below looked as if a bomb had been dropped on it. It was brown and flat as far as the doctor could see. Not a single tree was standing.

"It's gone," a small, sad voice beside him choked. "Everything I own. Gone."

Dr. Dolittle looked down at the heartsick squirrel at his feet. And at that moment he knew he had to help the forest creatures. Squaring his shoulders, he thought, *I will not let them down.*

Right away, Dr. Dolittle called his wife, Lisa, to ask for legal advice.

"How do you even save a forest?" he asked her from his cell phone, surveying the leveled land around him.

"It's not easy," she told him. "The lumber companies have a lot of clout." She paused for a moment. "But," she went on, "if there's a threatened or endangered species living in the forest, there are laws that protect it."

Dolittle thoughtfully tugged at his mustache. "How can I find out if there are any endangered animals?" he asked.

"Ask Eugene," Lisa suggested.

The doctor winced. "Not Eugene." It wasn't that he disliked Eugene. He wasn't a bad person. Far from it, in fact. It was just that sometimes he could be . . . a little much. But he was also a good friend—to the Dolittles and to animals.

Groaning, Dolittle thanked his wife and said goodbye. Then he made a call in to his office and told his secretary to cancel the day's appointments. His patients could wait. The forest could not. Taking a deep breath, he dialed the number of zoologist Eugene Wilson.

Not surprisingly, when Dolittle called Eugene, he found that his friend was already familiar with the situation. And by the time Dolittle met him at the San Francisco Zoo, Eugene had already researched endangered species in the region and was ready with a report.

Eugene and his friends had been trying for years to stop the huge lumber company, Potter Industries, from removing all the trees in the region—with no success. The company was just too big and too powerful, it seemed. The only forest still standing was the few hundred acres known as Campbell's Grove. But at the rate Potter was going with his clearcutting, it didn't look like the forest would be standing for long.

"Well, we found an endangered species of bear," Eugene told the doctor, his SAVE THE WHALES and SAVE THE EAGLES buttons dangling from his vest. "One female whose mother had been killed by poachers. She's the only Pacific Western bear up there."

He stroked the meerkat in his arms and straightened the SAVE THE OCEANS button on his lab coat.

"So that's good," Dolittle said eagerly. "One bear—she has to be protected."

The zoologist shook his head. "No—we already tried that. The lawyers for Potter's logging company argued that since she's the only one up there, there's no chance of the species surviving anyway. There'd have to be a male, too."

Dolittle tried to consider this—despite the loud, hissing giraffe pawing at the ground behind him.

"Okay," he said after a moment, "so let's get us a male bear up there. Get the two of them together, a little wine, a little Marvin Gaye, let nature take its course."

"Yo! Doc!" the giraffe called out rudely. "Yo!"

But Dolittle tuned him out and focused instead on Eugene's answer.

"Unfortunately, the only Pacific Western male we found has been raised in captivity." Eugene shook his head knowingly. "And there's never been a bear raised in captivity who's been introduced into the wild."

Dr. Dolittle smiled and pointed proudly to himself. "That's because you didn't have the world-famous love doctor making the introductions."

"Psst! Doc!"

"Excuse me," Dolittle finally said to his friend. He turned and walked over to the giraffe's enclosure. "Can I help you?" he asked, looking up into the animal's long face.

The giraffe stretched its graceful neck and whispered in the doctor's ear.

"Something wrong?" Eugene called from across the pen.

"A-hem." Dr. Dolittle cleared his throat uncomfortably and nodded toward the scientist's pants.

"Oh!" his zoologist friend exclaimed. Blushing, he quickly pulled up his zipper.

Then, blushing himself, Dr. Dolittle thanked his animal-loving friend and made his getaway before any more embarrassing situations arose. He did, after all, have important business to attend to. Somehow he had to *un*tame a tame bear enough so it could live—and reproduce—in the wild.

First, though, he had to do something even harder . . . explain to his teenage daughter that their European vacation would have to wait.

Chapter 5

That evening, Dr. Dolittle drove home as slowly as he could. Sooner or later, though, he knew he would have to face Charisse.

"Are you disappointed?" he asked after explaining to her and the rest of the family what he had to do.

"Disappointed?" Charisse laughed bitterly. "About not going to Europe?" She scowled as she tugged at the ruffles on her bedspread. "Why would I be disappointed? In Europe there'd just be a lot of glamour and excitement. But here I'd get to hang with Smokey the Bear."

Dolittle laid his arm across her shoulders. "Okay, okay," he said softly. "I made you a promise and I'll stick to it. If you don't want me to do this, I understand."

Charisse sighed and looked away. "Like I can really say no and not feel guilty the rest of my life."

"I'll make it up to you," her father promised.

"Please don't!" she snapped back.

"So when do we go?" Maya piped up.

Dolittle turned to his younger daughter. "As soon as we get a court order stopping the clear-cutting," he told her.

"Who's going to argue the case?" his wife asked.

Dolittle looked at her and grinned.

"No, no, no!" Lisa held up her hand and shook her head.

"Oh, come on, baby," Dolittle pleaded, knowing his wife couldn't really turn him down. "It's for the *environment*. . . ."

Within twenty-four hours, the brief was filed. And soon Lisa Dolittle was in the courtroom pleading the animals' case.

"We are asking for an injunction so that we might have the chance to save a species," she told the judge.

"Your Honor," countered Jack Riley, the attorney hired by Potter Industries, "it's a delaying tactic-slash-publicity stunt. I have affidavits from a range of experts who say that a bear raised in captivity *cannot* be successfully reintroduced into the wild. They don't know how to feed themselves, get along with other bears, let alone make it through a winter. It's . . . Darwin's law of nature. Survival of the fittest."

"Yeah." Suddenly Maya stood in her seat in the back of the room. "Well, Darwin never met my dad."

Stunned, the entire court turned around to see who had made the outburst.

The offended judge banged his gavel.

"And who is your father, young lady?" he asked sternly as the room returned to order.

"I am, Your Honor." Dr. Dolittle slowly rose to his feet beside his daughter. "The name's Dolittle."

"*Doctor* Dolittle," Maya added proudly.

An excited buzz filled the courtroom at the sound of the famous doctor's name. Even the judge was impressed.

Jack Riley groaned. "Oh, great."

"Dr. Dolittle," the judge inquired, ignoring the lawyer, "do *you* feel you can rehabilitate a tame bear and mate it in the wild to a female?"

The doctor nodded emphatically. "Yes," he answered, "I do."

The judge rubbed his dark-bearded chin for a moment. "In that case," he declared, "I will grant a one-month delay in the harvesting of Campbell's Grove. One month, Dr. Dolittle. That's it."

Dolittle's face broke into a broad grin. "Thank you, Your Honor," he said.

"And, Doctor." The judge held up his gavel with a

warning air. "If that bear so much as puts one paw into a campsite or this town, I'll rescind this order immediately."

"Yes, Your Honor." Dolittle nodded again. "I understand."

Smiling back at the doctor, the judge banged his gavel once more. Court was adjourned. And right away, the reporters swarmed.

They fired question after question at Dolittle.

"Where is this tame bear?"

"How are you going to retrain him?"

The doctor shrugged humbly and beamed into the TV cameras. "I know nothing about the bear," he admitted, "except that he lives in captivity, so I'm sure he'll be very happy to return to the wild."

That very evening, Dr. Dolittle drove out to meet the bear who was going to save the forest. Dolittle could hardly wait to tell him he would soon be free.

The address Eugene had given him said "Klondike Brown's Wild Animal Show." Strange, Dolittle thought, that he'd never heard of it. But when he got there, he could understand why. It was little more than a second-rate tourist-trap dinner theater a few hours outside of town. It looked like it could go out of business any minute, in fact, making Dolittle more certain than ever that he'd be doing the bear a favor.

What self-respecting bear would live this way by choice? At least that was what Dr. Dolittle thought when he sat down to watch the show.

"Okay, everybody," the bear trainer announced to the sparse audience, "before we bring out the main attraction, let me just remind you all that even trained bears are still wild animals—please do not make any sudden movements or loud noises that could provoke him." He cleared his throat and gazed around at the unimpressed crowd. "And now, ladies and gentlemen, how 'bout a big howdy-do for Archie, the biggest, baddest bear this side of the Mississippi!"

There was a round of weak applause and a few giggles from the back row—as in came a bear wearing a loud, moth-eaten vest and riding an old, dented scooter.

"Look at them," the bear said to himself as he waved to the bored spectators. "They love me! They worship me! I am a god!"

Then he caught a whiff of something sweet . . . salty . . . yummy. . . . He licked his chops. "Is that peanut butter? No, wait, Archie," he told himself, "focus!"

The bear passed once around the ring, then rode straight out toward the audience.

"Born to be wiii . . . *AAAAH!*"

With a heavy thud, the bear tumbled off his scooter and careened into the cassette player.

The taped music came to a grinding halt. But with

a "show-must-go-on" pump of his paw, the bear climbed back onto his scooter, kicked his hind paw, and—fell again, knocking over some scenery.

Awkwardly Archie picked up his scooter and ambled toward the edge of the stage.

"Thank you!" he called happily. "Good night! Remember your waiters!"

After the show had finished, Dr. Dolittle followed Archie to his backstage dressing room.

While the bear soaked in an herbal bubble bath, the doctor tried to explain why exactly he was there. To put it bluntly, Dolittle told him, the whole future of the forest—and its innocent inhabitants—depended on him and just one other bear. . . .

"Kind of a big-boned gal," Archie mused as he examined the wild bear Ava's picture. "Do you have any action shots?"

Just then a gaudily costumed chicken with cymbals on his legs clanged by.

"Great show, man," he called in a gravelly voice.

"Thanks." Archie waved and nodded. Then he turned back to the photo. He still didn't look convinced.

"You know, you'd be lucky to get someone like her," the doctor said, trying to sell him on the plan.

"Well." The bear adjusted his shower cap. "I haven't had a girlfriend in, uh . . . ever, honestly. Tell you what," he said at last, "bring her by. I'm dark on Mondays."

"No, no, no." Dr. Dolittle shook his head. "You're going to *her*."

"Going to her where?"

"The forest," said the doctor.

"I don't play forests," the bear explained. "I'm strictly a state fair, small arena–type bear."

Dolittle slipped the photo back into his pocket. "Archie," he said slowly, "do you know what kind of bear you are?"

"Yes, I do." The bear flashed a practiced grin. "I'm a singer, a dancer, I do impressions."

"No, look." Dr. Dolittle leaned in closer. "You're an endangered species."

"Is that a threat?" Archie looked worried. "I don't want any trouble."

The doctor groaned. "Shut up for a second, will you? You're a Pacific Western bear."

"Yeah, but I can play any kind of bear. Grizzly, panda, polar. I've got range."

"No," Dolittle said patiently, trying to make himself perfectly clear. "Your ancestors lived in the mountains of California. When you were six months old, they took you away from your mother to teach you how to wiggle your hips to a recording of 'Hound Dog.'"

Archie frowned and shook his head. "No, I taught myself that." He shrugged. "I admit, I pander. I'm a *pander* bear." He chuckled. "Get it?"

Dolittle forced a polite smile. "I do. But let's be serious for a moment. . . . I'm taking you back to the forest where your ancestors roamed." With both hands, he clasped the bear's furry forearm. "I'm going to teach you how to be a bear."

Archie tugged his paw away. "But I like the bear I am," he argued. "I'm famous. Have you been in the gift shop? I have my own plush toy."

"What *I'm* talking about," Dolittle told him, "would make you the most famous bear in the world."

Archie considered the idea for a moment. "Bigger than Pooh?" he said, arching his brow.

"You pull this off," the doctor assured him, "I guarantee you it'll be 'Winnie the *Who?*'"

Little by little, a smile spread across Archie's face. And with a nod toward the future, man and bear shook hand and paw.

Chapter 6

Meanwhile, all over San Francisco, Dr. Dolittle and his scheme were all anyone could talk about. And Mr. Joseph Potter himself was no exception. As the owner of Potter Industries, he had everything to gain from seeing Campbell's Grove plowed down—and everything to lose if Dolittle's plan was a success.

As far as Potter was concerned, he had no choice. He had to stop Dolittle—any way he could. Which was why he called the governor of California to meet him at his office at the crack of dawn.

Silently, they watched yet another news report on the famous doctor:

"In what must be one of the most unusual stories this year, Dr. John Dolittle is trying to rewrite the laws of nature by attempting to reintroduce a performing bear into the wild. And in doing so, he hopes to save an entire forest from destruction. It's Darwin versus Dolittle . . ."

Potter angrily grabbed the remote control and turned off the TV.

"Governor," he growled, "I've got two lumber mills waiting for that wood."

"I understand, Joe," Elston Cartwright replied. He loosened his tie and looked around the businessman's expansive office—feeling as helpless as one of the stuffed animal heads lining the wood-paneled walls.

"But it's complicated," Governor Cartwright went on, "especially if that endangered bear survives."

Potter's already small eyes narrowed. "I don't meet my quota, Governor, you're the one who's going to be endangered."

He had bullied the governor into bending laws for him before. And he'd do it again if he had to. After all, both he and Cartwright knew he could buy and sell the state. And he could always put another governor in place—one who'd help him.

As the governor stood by looking uncomfortable, Jack Riley stepped forward and smiled.

"Don't worry, Mr. Potter," the lawyer reassured his boss. "That bear's going to slip up once and when he does, we'll be there."

Potter rubbed his hands together greedily and

gazed at an empty patch of wall between two hunting trophies.

"And I've got just the place to put him," he sneered.

That same morning, Dr. Dolittle set out to commune with nature—with his family and his showbiz bear in tow.

They drove through the California mountains until at last they reached the rustic cabin in the forest where they'd be spending the next few weeks. And out in front were the beaver and his friends, waiting eagerly to greet them.

"Okay, everybody," Dolittle announced to the animals as they gathered around, "you all know why we're here. We're about to do something that has never been done before. Everyone out there doesn't think we can do it. They've got their blades sharpened and their trucks ready to roll. We're going to prove them wrong."

"Yeah! Word! You bet!" the animals cheered.

"And now," said the doctor, stepping around to the back of his truck, "I want you to meet the bear who's going to help lead the way. Say hello to Archie!"

Dolittle yanked open the door and stood back as Archie sprang out.

"Are you ready to save the forest?" the bear shouted. "Put your paws together!"

Archie clapped his own paws together heartily . . . but his audience did not.

"I know you're out there," he joked with them. "I can hear you shedding. Ha, ha."

He waited for a round of laughter—and when it didn't come, he crouched down beside a squirrel.

"Hi there!" he bantered. "Where you from?"

The squirrel stared back at him blankly. "*Here. We're all from here.*"

Archie awkwardly stood up and cleared his throat. If he'd had a tie, he would have loosened it—but the doc had said no fancy costumes.

"You're losing them," Dolittle whispered out of the corner of his mouth.

You're telling me, the bear thought. But he'd faced tougher crowds before.

"I want to go serious on you for a second," he said, trying out a different tone. "I know I've got my work cut out for me. But with your help, I know one thing."

Archie pulled out a portable tape player, and when the pop music began, he started to sway.

He began to sing the chorus of "I Will Survive."

Unimpressed and uninspired, the animals turned to go.

"*For as long as I know how to love I know I'll stay alive!*"

The beaver paused in front of Dolittle and sadly shook his head. "We're dead."

"You're not a real bear, are you?" Dr. Dolittle asked Archie after the forest animals had scattered. He tugged on the bear's shaggy shoulder. "You're Wayne Newton in a bear suit."

Archie, however, was concerned with something else. "It's so dirty," he whined, lifting up a padded foot. "Look at my paws."

"It's called *the woods,* Archie," the doctor groaned as he began to walk away. "Its main component is dirt." He was beginning to get the feeling that *he* had a better chance of making it in the forest than this blow-dried prima donna.

"Hey, Doc!" Archie's voice suddenly called out.

"What?"

"Is that her? She's a babe!"

Dolittle swung around to find Archie gawking at the forest. He followed the bear's gaze and spotted a hefty, glossy-furred female bear rooting among the trees.

"Look at the way she moves!" Archie panted. "Oh, man, would I love to see her wet!"

Dr. Dolittle's face lit up. It had to be Ava!

"Wait here a second," he told Archie, who was snorting appreciatively. "I'll go over and introduce you."

"Yeah!" the bear responded. "Tell her I really dig her fat pouch, but don't be crude."

"I'll try to work it in," Dolittle said dryly.

Trying to look cool, the doctor strolled up to the blackberry bush the bear was picking through.

"How's it going?" he asked casually. "I'm John."

"I'm Ava," she replied between pawfuls.

"Ava." Dr. Dolittle moved in a little closer. "How would you like to meet the man of your dreams?"

She looked away and turned up her nose. "Look, you seem very nice, but I don't go interspecies."

"Not me!" Dolittle waved his hands and laughed. Then he nodded back toward the path. "Do you see that magnificent hunk of he-bear?"

Ava followed his gaze. "No." She shook her head. "Is he standing behind the dork?"

"No, he *is* the—" Dr. Dolittle cleared his throat. "Look, let me explain why he's here. A logging company is going to rip down this whole forest. The only way to stop them is if two Pacific Western bears, uh . . . hook up and create little Pacific Western bears." He paused for a moment. "See where I'm going with this?"

"See where *I'm* going," she answered as she began to lumber off.

"Wait!" called Dr. Dolittle. "At least let me bring him over here so you can meet him." Then he hurried back to Archie.

"You're on," he told the bear.

Archie looked at him, petrified. "What do I say to her?" he asked timidly.

"Just let her get to know you. Tell her a little about yourself." Then he gave the bear a push in Ava's direction.

Archie made his way to Ava's side. She looked bored and annoyed, and seconds from walking away. Still, Archie took a deep breath and gave his come-on his best shot. He was, after all, an *actor,* wasn't he?

"Hi," he gulped, forcing an optimistic grin. "I'm Archie. I like moonlit walks on the beach, sharing a slop bucket with that special someone, and the soulful sounds of the Backstreet Boys."

Ava looked at his big brown eyes with pity and a touch of fear. "You are seriously weird," she replied.

"Weird as in 'sexy'?" he asked.

"Weird as in 'go away.'"

Dr. Dolittle walked up and patted the speechless bear on the shoulder. "Uh, good work, Archie. I'll take it from here."

Crushed, Archie slumped off down the path while the doctor tried to repair the damage he had done.

"So." He turned to Ava and smiled. "What do you think of Archie?"

"I think it's the first time I've ever wanted to see a bear shot," she answered, curling her lip in disgust.

"Look, he's just a little nervous around women, but—"

"That's not the point," Ava broke in. "I need a real bear! Someone who can hunt and protect and provide for me."

"You know," said Dolittle patiently, "that's not very millennium. Nowadays women provide for themselves. My wife's a very successful lawyer."

"I don't see myself making that career move," the bear replied. "And besides . . ." She pawed at the ground. "I'm already involved with someone."

"But do you love him?" Dolittle asked.

"Love? Look, my cousin married for love, and the next thing she knows, he's two-timing her with this hot little grizzly in a cave up north."

"Let me make a deal with you," Dolittle suggested. "Don't make any decisions for a month. I'll work with Archie and I promise you, I'll turn him into the kind of bear you'd be proud to have cubs with."

Ava looked at him skeptically. Slowly her expression began to soften . . .

. . . until suddenly Archie vaulted into the berry patch, did a handstand, and tumbled over.

"I've flipped for you!" he called, beaming at the dumbstruck bear.

Ava glared at him and then at Dr. Dolittle. Then she turned with a grunt and angrily waddled off.

Chapter 7

Dr. Dolittle had known he had a lot of work cut out for him. But he'd never imagined he would have to start from scratch! He just hoped he hadn't ruined his chances by having Archie talk to Ava. The spoiled bear clearly wasn't ready to court a wild woman. But at least now Dolittle knew what Ava was looking for in a mate: a "real bear." And that was exactly what she was going to get.

It was time to begin Archie's crash course in Wild Bear 101. And what better place to start than with good old nature TV?

Dolittle and Archie sat in the cabin. On the large screen in front of them, a huge male grizzly turned over a log and rooted around for grubs.

"Bears are opportunistic eaters, finding food wherever they can," the narrator droned on.

Archie tried not to gag. "Can we see what else is on?" he asked from his seat on the couch beside the doctor. He took another pawful of buttered popcorn.

"No!" Dolittle scolded. "This is the stuff you need to learn. How to feed yourself. How to survive the winter. So just be quiet and watch."

Obediently, Archie focused on the screen, where a black bear was now climbing nimbly up a tree.

"Wow. How'd he get up there?" Archie asked, amazed.

"Haven't you ever wondered what your sharp claws are for?" Dolittle asked, pointing to Archie's front and hind paws.

"No, not really." Archie shrugged, tossing a piece of popcorn in the air and trying to catch it in his mouth.

"Bears are excellent swimmers," the narrator went on as another bear jumped into a river and pulled out a fish.

"Not this bear," Archie said, shaking his head.

"Don't tell me you don't know how to swim!" Dolittle exclaimed.

"I can run through sprinklers. With a nose plug."

"Okay," said Dolittle matter-of-factly. "Tomorrow, you and I are getting up at the crack of dawn and I'm gonna teach you how to fish."

Archie groaned.

"Just watch," the doctor told him. "And learn."

Later that evening, Dr. Dolittle took a much-needed break from *un*training Archie to spend time with his family—and more specifically, Charisse.

He found his oldest daughter sulking out on the cabin's front porch steps. He could tell she was in the mood to be alone, but he sat down beside her anyway.

"See? Isn't this nice?" he said after a few awkward minutes. "Sitting out here in the country, listening to the crickets."

Charisse kept her head in her hands and shrugged.

"You know what they're saying?" Dolittle asked.

She flashed him a hot, almost guilty glare. "No!" she snapped. "No, I don't know what they're saying! You're the one who understands them. Not me."

"Whoa, easy there," her father told her. "I was just gonna say that crickets are nature's thermometers. They tell you the temperature based on how fast they chirp."

He listened for a moment.

"*Chirp* . . . *Chirp* . . . Fifty-eight degrees. Fifty-eight degrees. Fifty-eight degrees. Fifty-*five* degrees. Fifty-five degrees . . . *Chirp* . . ."

Charisse looked back down at the ground. Then she wrapped her arms around her shoulders.

"I'd better get a sweater," she said, heading for the cabin.

For a moment Dr. Dolittle wondered. . . . It almost seemed like Charisse had understood what the crickets were chirping. *Nah.* He shook his head. That was crazy. *He* was the only Dolittle who could talk to the animals.

With a sigh, he closed his eyes and breathed in the woodsy night air, trying his best to enjoy the moment—when a blast of hip-hop music suddenly shattered the peaceful night.

"What the . . . ?" the doctor muttered.

The next thing he knew, a convertible full of teenagers pulled up in front of the cabin. One of them climbed out.

"Eric!" Charisse shouted as she burst out of the front door she'd just entered.

To Dr. Dolittle's horror, she bounded past him, down the steps, and into her new boyfriend's waiting arms.

"Hey, baby!" Eric said fondly.

Grinning, he pulled some things out of the trunk and waved goodbye to his friends. Then he watched them drive away.

"I knew you'd miss the city," he told Charisse, "so I thought I'd bring a little of the city out to you." He handed her a pizza box and watched her lift the top.

In the box were a pizza and a long-stemmed red rose.

"You are the sweetest guy ever!" Charisse exclaimed. She threw her arms around his neck and planted an ecstatic kiss.

"Ah-hmmm." Watching grimly from the porch, Dr. Dolittle cleared his throat.

"Hey, Dr. D!" Eric called. "Whassup?"

"I don't know, Eric," Dolittle replied coldly. "Why don't *you* tell *me* whassup?"

Eric puffed out his chest, then winked at Charisse. "I came to visit. I'll be staying for a while."

"Oh . . . really? And who said you could stay for a while?" Dolittle asked.

"Mom did," Charisse answered.

"Oh, really?" Dr. Dolittle swallowed. "I see."

That settled things, Dolittle realized—but it didn't mean he had to like it!

"Fine," he grunted. "But I'm on to you, buddy." He wagged a finger threateningly at Eric. Then he turned toward the house.

"And remember," he called back over his shoulder to the two teens, "I have excellent night vision."

Before the sun had even risen, as his family slept soundly in their warm, quilt-covered bunk beds,

Dolittle dragged Archie outside to begin another day of lessons.

"This river's full of fish," he told the bear as he led him to the shore.

"So's Red Lobster," grunted Archie.

The bear stared blankly at the doctor. He clearly had no idea what to do next.

"Don't look at me," Dolittle told him. "Look in the water. That's where the fish are!"

Tentatively Archie lowered his head and peered in. "Oh my God," he exclaimed, "they're moving! Quick, sauté them!"

"Keep your voice down," the doctor whispered, clamping his hand over the bear's muzzle. "You'll scare the fish. Now listen, you two-ton furry baby." He pointed toward the rushing water. "Put your head in there and grab a fish."

"No," Archie muttered.

"Come on." Dolittle tugged impatiently on Archie's ear. "Like we saw on TV. Stick your head under the water and catch a fish!"

The bear's deep brown eyes narrowed. "All right," he finally growled. "I'll try it!"

"One . . . two . . ."

On the count of three, Archie took a deep breath, pinched his nose, and plunged his head into the water.

"Oh my God! It's a bear!"

Beneath the surface, the fish went crazy.

"Swim for your life!" they cried. "Quick, everybody upstream!"

Meanwhile, up above, Dr. Dolittle waited . . . and waited . . . and waited.

"Archie!"

Minutes later, Archie was laid out on the shore, and Dr. Dolittle was furiously performing emergency bear CPR.

"How smart do you have to be to take your head out of the water when you can't breathe?" he chided Archie when the bear finally came to.

"Oh, sure!" Archie fired back after spitting out a mouthful of river water. "Monday-morning quarterback!"

"All right, that's it!" Dr. Dolittle stood up and put his hands crossly on his hips. "We're going on a little trip to toughen you up."

"Where?" Archie asked, his eyes suddenly wide and nervous.

"It's a surprise."

Chapter 8

Desperate times called for desperate measures,
Dr. Dolittle knew. And he was done fooling around.

It was zoo time.

"What are we doing?" Archie asked as the doctor
led him down a row of cold iron cages. Dolittle had
driven him out to the county's zoological park that
morning. "It's time for a little tough love," Dolittle
replied. He stopped in front of a set of doors and motioned for a guard to unlock them.

With a rusty squeak, the bars swung open, reveal-
ing two tough-looking bears sitting in a cramped,
bleak exhibit.

"Go on in." The doctor nodded.

Archie hung back. "Why?" he asked.

"Coupla bears want to meet you."

Then Dolittle gave him a helpful shove.

The zoo-hardened bears sized up Archie as he stumbled into their cell.

"Couldn't make it on the outside?" one of the tough guys asked.

"Couldn't say no to that two-legged baldy," the other teased, nodding toward the doctor.

"Uhhh . . ." Archie cowered by the door and watched the bears stand up and begin to cross the cage.

"Locked up for life," the first bear said proudly. "Doin' hard time!"

The second bear shot Archie a cold, snaggle-toothed snarl. "You wanna spend the rest of your life in the big house too?"

"Be our guest," said the first, "and when we're done with you, we'll sell you to the grizzly in C-block for a carton of berries."

Outside the cage, Dr. Dolittle was smiling. Inside, Archie was trembling. The doc's plot to scare him straight seemed to be going well.

Beeeep. Beeeep.

The doctor pulled out his cell phone and clicked it on.

"Dolittle . . . Hi, honey. No, it's going well. . . . Yeah, I think I've got it all under control. . . ."

"Ha, ha . . . *ha!*"

The air around him was suddenly filled with laughter.

Dolittle looked puzzled. "I'll call you back, Lisa," he said into the phone.

He hung up and peered through the bars into the cage.

"We are family . . . ," Archie was singing.

"I've got all my sisters with me," the bears chimed in, doing backup moves behind him.

Dr. Dolittle buried his face in his hands. "Don't tell me," he moaned.

It was back to the drawing board once again!

One week was almost up, and Dr. Dolittle was getting nervous. But he wasn't letting on—not to Archie or anyone else.

"How's it going?" Lisa asked him as they ate lunch on the porch.

"Great!" Dolittle answered a little too enthusiastically. "It's going great! I won't even need three more weeks. I mean, look at him." He waved his arm in Archie's direction. "He's foraging for grapes right now."

The family turned to watch as Archie hopelessly sniffed around a nearby tree. He had no idea the grapes he was looking for were hanging right over his head.

"No offense, Doc," Eric said with a chuckle, "but e's dumber than the average bear."

Meanwhile, Lucky and Pepito were trying to help bear as best they could.

"Cold," Lucky barked as Archie began to waddle away.

"*Frio,*" squeaked the lizard.

"Arctic," Lucky went on.

"Why is he walking away from them?" Eric asked Dolittle.

The doctor chewed on his lip for a moment. "He's circling them," he said at last.

"Why?" asked Charisse. "Are they dangerous grapes?"

"Chilly," Pepito said, giving a mock shiver. "*Muy* chilly."

"Don't worry." Dolittle frowned and picked up his egg salad sandwich. "We are right on schedule. He's doing great!"

Thud—thu-thu-thump!

The rest of the family winced as Archie backed up—right into the open storm cellar. And they tried not to laugh as Dr. Dolittle choked on his lunch.

"I'm okay," called Archie from the bottom of the steps. "The concrete broke my fall."

"Man!" Eric told Dolittle as he peered into the hole. "Those grapes kicked your bear's butt!"

Enough foraging, Dolittle quickly decided. There was more to being a real bear, after all.

That afternoon, he took Archie out to find an

empty bear den. And when they found an empty tree stump, the doctor had Archie look in.

"Now, explain this again," the bear said, scratching his head. "I'm supposed to climb into a small, dark space and sleep for six months?"

"That's right. It's called hibernation."

"Sounds more like depression," grumbled Archie. "How do I eat and drink?"

"You don't," replied the doctor. "You eat enough during the summer to last the whole winter."

The bear thought the idea over for a minute. "Where do I go to the bathroom?" he asked.

"You don't," said Dolittle.

The bear laughed. "Very funny."

"I'm serious," Dolittle told him. "The last week before you hibernate, you'll start eating hair, dirt, moss, grass—it forms a plug that blocks your . . . you know."

Archie shook his head. "I don't."

Dolittle fiddled with his mustache. "The place on your body that allows you to go . . ."

"Go where?"

"Not where," said Dolittle. "*To*. As in . . . go *to* the bathroom."

Archie's neck fur suddenly bristled. "It blocks it ?"

"Yeah." The doctor nodded.

"Big job or little job?"

"Big job," Dolittle answered.

When Dr. Dolittle talks, the animals listen!

Dolittle loves a
good audience.

Eric is finding out a little too much information about Charisse!

These rats *weren't* invited to the party.

Lisa Dolittle.

The judge gives Dolittle a chance to save the forest.

Archie checks out Ava's picture. Hmmm . . .

Trying to teach Archie Wild Bear 101.

Everyone's worried . . . will Archie
be able to survive in the wild?

Learning to walk the walk.

Romance, Dolittle-style.

Pepito is about to say something to Maya, isn't he?

Is it all over for Archie and Dolittle?

Archie held up his paws and shook his head like a wet dog. "So let me get this straight. You want me to sleep for six months with a big hairy . . ." He gulped. ". . . thing in my . . ." He winced. ". . . thing."

"That's the idea," the doctor replied.

To Dr. Dolittle's dismay, Archie fell to all fours and began to run away.

"Archie, get back here!" Dolittle shouted.

"You'll have to kill me first," the bear called back.

It took a good half hour for Dolittle to catch up with Archie on the highway. Lucky for him the bear wasn't in the greatest shape.

"Archie." He sighed after another car drove past. "Nobody's going to pick up a hitchhiking bear."

"I'll split gas," Archie replied with determination, stubbornly keeping his thumbless paw in the air. "I'll sit in the back with the kids."

"Archie, come on."

But the bear shook his head. "Sorry, Doc, this just isn't working out. I almost drowned, Ava doesn't like me—"

"I'm sick of you and your complaining," Dolittle broke in. "Look up in that tree." He pointed to a sturdy elm. "What do you see?"

Archie stopped and lifted his head. "A bird," he said.

Dolittle nodded. "That's right. A bird in his home. And who's on that branch below him? A squirrel, also in his home. And see that rabbit by the fence? Every single one of them is depending on you. And you can do it. And all you have to do is learn to listen to your inner bear." He gently tapped on Archie's chest. "He'll tell you what to do. You just have to trust him."

Slowly Archie let his paw fall.

"What about the hairy, dirty plug?" he pouted as Dolittle led him back into the forest.

The doctor smiled. "Maybe there's a pill you can take."

Chapter 9

From then on, it was as if Archie were a different bear—and more like a *real* bear than ever. He went for runs with Dolittle. Climbed trees with Dolittle. He even caught a fish (after Dolittle promised the little guy he'd let him go). The doctor still hadn't managed to get Archie to eat grubs. But Dolittle knew it was only a matter of time.

After a week of camping out, in fact, Archie wasn't even afraid of dirt anymore. But something was still lying heavily on his mind.

"You seem a little sad," Dolittle said as they sat around the campfire making s'mores one evening.

"Well, I guess I sort of miss doing my act," the bear confessed.

"All right." Dolittle leaned back. "Let's say you

spend the rest of your life in show business. Where's your finish? Every act has to have its finish."

"I had a finish," Archie told him. "I used to do a full split like James Brown. *Haiiiii!*"

"No," Dolittle explained, motioning for Archie to sit back down. "I mean in your life. Who are you going to share your success with? Your failures, your fears, your hopes?" He pointed to himself. "All I do would mean nothing to me if I couldn't come home to Lisa and the girls."

Archie's shaggy head drooped. "Sometimes I do get very lonely," he sniffed. "I've never been in love."

"Now's your chance," the doctor told him. "I think Ava likes you."

Archie's head sprang up. "What? Did she say something? What did she say?"

"Say?" Dolittle chewed on his lip. "She, uh . . . sometimes you have to read between the lines," he finally said with a weak smile.

"She loves me!" Archie roared. "I knew it!"

"Let's not get carried away," Dolittle said as he tried to dodge Archie's waving marshmallow.

"I feel like I'm about to burst!" Archie went on. "So this is what love feels like . . . *brrrurppp!*" He rubbed his belly. "Or maybe it's the marshmallows."

While Archie settled down, Dolittle stowed the marshmallows and graham crackers and poured his cold coffee on the fire.

"Night," he said as he headed toward his tent.

"Don't go," the bear called softly. "It's a little scary out here for me." He batted his eyes. "Stay here till I fall asleep."

"Okay." The doctor nodded.

He sat down once more next to Archie, and couldn't help smiling as he watched him fall asleep. Then he quietly stood up and grabbed a pail to douse the fire.

"Hey, Doc," Archie murmured, "can you leave the light on?"

"Sure." The doctor smiled again and set the water down.

"Sweet dreams, Archie," he said.

The next day, the tutorials continued.

"Now listen," Dr. Dolittle told the bear as Lucky watched. "What every female looks for is the strongest male."

"But what about personality?" Archie asked.

Dolittle brusquely shook his head. "There is in nature," he explained, "something called the alpha male." He held up his first finger. "The number one, man's man male, who shows everybody he's the boss. You have to learn to walk the walk."

With that, Dolittle began to strut across the mossy yard. Then he stopped and waited for Archie to follow.

"Walk the walk," Archie echoed, awkwardly waddling along.

"And talk the talk," Dolittle went on in a deep, manly-man voice.

"I'm still on the walk," Lucky protested.

But the doctor was in his alpha-male zone. "It's all about respect," he went on, caught up in the moment. "It's about authority! It's about power! Unchecked, uncompromised, testosterone-driven male power!"

"John," Dolittle's wife suddenly called from the cabin door, "didn't I ask you to line the garbage pails?"

"Do that yourself, woman!" he impatiently yelled back.

"What?" shouted Lisa.

"Uh—" All of a sudden Dr. Dolittle's testosterone-driven shoulders drooped as he realized exactly what he'd done.

"I'm taking care of it right now, sweetie," he called to his wife meekly.

"I thought you were going to town to get us some food!" Lisa snapped back with a furious glare.

"I'm on my way, honey."

"Way to go, big guy," Lucky barked.

"Shut up!" Dolittle hissed.

"Who are you telling to shut up?" Lisa called out.

"Not you, baby." And without looking at Archie, Dolittle dashed into the house to get his keys.

Later that day, after his chores were done, the doctor took Archie out for a walk in the woods before supper (with Lisa's permission, of course). He was hoping they'd see Ava again—and they did see her, basking in the last rays of the sun among the wild-flowers and clover.

"How can anyone be so beautiful?" Archie sighed.

"Go down there and tell her that," Dolittle urged him.

But before Archie could gather his courage, another bear lumbered up to Ava's side. He was enormous, and good-looking in a wild, primitive way. Archie disliked him on first scent.

"Who's *that*?" he asked, annoyed.

"Oh," said the doctor, peering down. "That must be Sonny. He's . . . Ava's boyfriend." He turned to see Archie's dumbstruck face.

"Don't worry," Dolittle assured him, "you can win her away from him. The key to winning a woman is figuring out what she wants. Take my wife—"

"Please," Archie cut in, unable to resist the worn-out joke.

"Don't do that," Dolittle warned.

"Sorry."

"Anyway," Dolittle went on, "my wife likes it when I surprise her."

"You mean by leaping out of the bushes and screaming?"

"No." Dolittle closed his eyes and heaved a sigh. "I mean with something romantic. Something unexpected. Something that says, 'I'm thinking about you all the time.'"

"That's really nice." Archie smiled. "Do you do that for your wife a lot?"

"I used to." Dolittle nodded. He paused and realized that it had been months since his last surprise.

"I guess I've been so caught up in other things that I kind of got out of practice," he said more to himself than to his companion.

Then he slowly turned to Archie.

"My friend," he said as his eyes lit up with an idea, "I think you need another night of camping."

Chapter 10

"John, what are you doing?" Lisa asked that evening as she walked into the cabin's living room.

There was a fire in the fireplace, a picnic blanket on the floor, wine and cheese, softly glowing candles everywhere, and her husband in a bathrobe, grinning from ear to ear.

"Baby, tonight's all about you," Dolittle said softly as he slipped in a CD. "The kids are at the movies and the bear's camping out in the woods. We're all alone."

"Yes, all alone!" He heard Pepito's lizardy voice snickering.

"Excuse me," the doctor told Lisa, blowing her a little kiss.

Then he stood up and crossed to the sofa.

"You cannot find me!" Pepito's voice teased. "I have blended *perfectly* into the couch!"

Frowning, the doctor lifted a throw blanket and stared down at the chameleon, which was still bright green.

"Oops," gulped Pepito, looking around at the plaid upholstery.

"Found ya," said Dolittle. He scooped Pepito up and carried him to the cage in Maya's room.

Meanwhile, Lucky saw Archie walking back from his campsite to the cabin.

"Show's about to start," he said with a wink to the puzzled bear.

"What show?" asked Archie.

Lucky trotted up to the living room window and pulled himself up on his hind legs.

"Just watch," he said as he nodded Archie over.

Inside, Dr. Dolittle was stretching himself out on the blanket. "Now, where were we?" he said, looking up at Lisa.

She held back and tried her best to hide her smile. "You were thinking a few candles and some wine would make up for ignoring me these past few days."

"Ooh." Dolittle held up his hands. "I'm sensing a little resistance." He wagged his finger. "You may be able to resist the magnificent piece of man before you, my dear, but there's no way you can resist . . ." He held up the stereo remote control. "Lionel."

With a click, Lisa's favorite love song began to play, and Dr. Dolittle began to croon with the music.

"Truuuly, truly in love with you, girl."

He reached his arms out to his wife . . . and, laughing, she walked toward him.

"Oh, he's so good," Archie whispered to Lucky as they spied on Dolittle through the window.

"What's going on?" a deep voice asked.

Archie glanced over his shoulder to see the beaver and several friends assembled on the grass behind them.

"Apparently, he's truly, truly in love with her, girl," the bear replied.

"Hey, Doc!" the raccoon called out, pulling himself up to the window. "Bring her some trash! No woman can resist trash!"

"Shhh!" whispered Lucky.

Fascinated, the animals watched as the doctor stood up and began to dance cheek to cheek with Lisa. "Hey, baby," Dolittle said, nuzzling her ear. "You're looking mighty fine. So why don't you plant some of that sugar over here?"

"Go, Doctor! Go, Doctor!" they chanted, and pumped their paws.

Oblivious, Dolittle spun his wife around and dipped her over his knee . . . and finally spotted the Peeping Toms mashed against his window.

"Hey!" he shouted at the animals, and with a jolting thud dropped Lisa.

"Oh, no!" exclaimed the bobcat. "He broke her!"

"Run!" cried the raccoon.

Within seconds, Dolittle was on the porch, waving his fist wildly.

"Get out of here!" he shouted. "All of you! Go!"

Reluctantly the animals scattered—all except Archie.

"This ain't no show," the doctor barked at him.

"But it's really helpful," Archie said. "I'm learning a lot."

Dolittle clenched his jaw and pointed toward the forest. "Go," he grunted. "We'll discuss it tomorrow."

Disappointed, Archie turned and obediently began to walk away.

"You're going to *tell* him about this *tomorrow*?"

Lisa's angry voice made Dolittle spin around.

The doctor shook his head. "No, I mean, what I meant was . . ." He gulped and tried to bring back the romantic mood that had been stolen. "Hey, baby," he crooned, "why don't we pick up where we left off?"

"Hey, baby," Lisa huffed as she stomped back into the cabin, "why don't you sleep on the couch?"

And with that, she slammed the door.

"What'd she say?" Archie called back from the edge of the forest.

Dolittle grumbled to himself but tried to save face before his pupil. "She says she loves me so much, I get to sleep on the couch!"

"You're the *man!*" Archie whooped. Suddenly he felt much, much better. Maybe there was hope for him and Ava after all. Clearly he was learning from the master! How could he go wrong?

The next morning, full of confidence, Archie set off in search of Ava. He was determined to give this courtship thing another shot.

He found her easily enough, nosing through the berry bushes. Trying not to let his nerves show, he moved into the thicket and leaned against a skinny tree.

Archie cleared his throat. "Hey, baby," he announced in his best sexy Dr. Dolittle voice.

Ava looked over, unimpressed. "What do you want?"

"You're looking mighty fine," Archie told her, using the same line Dolittle had used on Lisa. "So why don't you plant some of that sugar over here?"

Ava stared at him for a second. Then she burst out laughing.

"Ha, ha, *ha-ha-ha!*" she howled in his face—just as the spindly birch collapsed under Archie's half-ton weight.

"*Ha-ha-HA!*" Ava grabbed her generous belly as tears began to fill her eyes.

That's it, Archie told himself as he watched her trot away. *I give up.*

Chapter 11

"**Archie, come out,**" Dolittle called into the hollow tree.

"Never," the bear muttered back.

Dolittle sighed. The raccoon had told him there was something wrong with Archie. But this was . . . bad!

"I'm sure it wasn't so bad," Dolittle lied.

"It was the most humiliating thing I've ever done," the bear replied. "And I once rode a unicycle in a tutu. A *tutu!*"

"I understand," Dolittle told him. "But we can fix it. We just have to work a little harder."

"Nope," Archie said. "I'm just going to stay here and hibernate."

Dolittle sighed again and slumped down against the tree.

"He's hopeless, isn't he?" Joey the raccoon said from his seat on a nearby rock.

The doctor glanced over at him. "Archie's fine," he lied once more.

"I guess we should start packing." This time it was the beaver speaking from atop a weathered stump.

"Nonsense," Dolittle told him. He rubbed his hands together. "It's all under control."

Of course, in his mind he knew it wasn't. It was completely *out* of control. That bear had quit on him. On all of them. And after they had come so close! But if Archie thought he was getting off the hook so easily, he was wrong. Dead wrong!

Fuming, Dr. Dolittle gritted his teeth and leaned back over Archie's hole. "Get out here, you coward. *Now!*" he yelled.

In a moment Archie emerged from the hollow tree.

"Who you callin' a coward?" he demanded.

"You, ya coward!" Dolittle answered. "Giving up like this."

"Well, it's hard," Archie pouted.

"It's *hard*? You wanna talk hard? Try being me. My daughter's mad at me. My wife's mad at me. I'm spending my vacation with a Snoop Doggy Dogg wannabe. . . . 'Yo, yo, Dr. D, whassup?' " he mimicked Eric. "And now I'm listening to a six-hundred-pound crybaby telling me he wants to quit because 'it's hard.' " Dolittle rolled his eyes in disgust.

"Well . . ." The bear sniffed and pawed the ground. "Ava laughed at me."

"Oh, boo-hoo," replied Dolittle, sarcastically pretending to cry. " 'I love her, I want her, she laughed at me.' You don't deserve Ava!" he told the bear with a stiff poke in the chest.

"Hey, don't poke the bear, buddy," Archie warned.

"Poking the bear? I'm not poking a bear. Because if I poked a bear, he'd maul me. So I don't know what I'm poking, but it sure ain't no bear." And with that, the doctor poked Archie again.

"I'm warning you. . . ." An angry growl rumbled up through Archie's throat.

"Yeah, and I'm poking you."

"Stop it!" Archie roared.

"Poke, poke, poke." The doctor jabbed at the bear's chest even more.

"All right." Archie's lips curled and foam bubbled around the corners of his mouth. "That's *it*!"

Furious, the bear reached out and gave Dolittle a mighty shove—sending the doctor flying into a huge puddle of mud.

"Dad." Just then Charisse came walking into the

clearing. "Mom wants to see you," she announced. Then she spotted her mud-packed father on all fours and stopped.

"What's going on?" she said, almost afraid to ask.

Dr. Dolittle stood up and wiped the mud off his glasses. "I'm whuppin' this bear's butt, that's what's going on," he stated.

"Oh, you want some more?" Archie taunted. "Let's go, cowboy!"

The doctor lunged for the bear, but his daughter held him back.

"Daddy, what are you doing?" she cried. "We didn't come out here so you could fight with a bear."

Dolittle unclenched his fists. "All right," he muttered. "I'll let you off the hook this time," he told Archie. "Lucky for you my daughter's here. Come on, Charisse." And he turned to go.

"That's it," called Archie. "Just run away!"

Dolittle kept his back to the bear and continued walking. "I'm not running away," he declared. "I'm walking away. I'm done with you."

"Fine!" Archie grunted. "I don't need your help!"

"No, you're *beyond* my help!" the doctor yelled as he and Charisse marched on. "Go back to the circus, Archie!"

Dr. Dolittle returned to the cabin with Charisse, completely unsure of what he was going to do next. Well, naturally he'd find out what his wife had wanted first. Then he'd shower and put on clean clothes. *But then what?* he asked himself. Archie could let the whole forest down if he wanted. But he, Dr. John Dolittle, had made a promise, and he was going to keep it, whatever he had to do.

"What happened to you?" Lisa asked as he walked through the door.

Dolittle stopped to take off his mud-caked shoes. "Me and Archie were making mud pies," he grumbled.

Then he noticed his wife's anxious face. "What's up?" he asked.

"Potter called," she told him. "I think he wants to make a deal."

Dolittle started toward the bathroom, shaking his muddy head. "No deals," he said.

"John—" Lisa began.

"I have another week," Dolittle told her. "I'll think of something."

"But John, it's not working! At least listen to what they have to say."

Then she offered the doctor the phone and Mr. Potter's number and waited for him to take them.

While Dolittle talked to Potter, Archie stomped around the forest, gradually cooling off. He was still as mad as a bear at a Goldilocks convention—that doctor had no business poking him and calling him a quitter. That hurt! Who was the real quitter, anyway? Archie wondered angrily. Dolittle was the one who had just walked away. . . .

All of a sudden Archie spied something and his anger melted away. Ava.

"Quitter, my paw!" he growled to himself as he charted a course for the stream. This bear was gonna catch him some fish . . . and who knew what else!

Thwuppp.

Ava reared back as a glistening trout landed, flopping, at her feet. Startled, she looked up to see where it had come from.

"For you, madame," Archie said, moseying up with a smile.

Ava flashed him a skeptical look, then leaned over to have a taste.

Mmm . . . not bad. "Thanks," she said, and licked her chops.

"So does *Sonny* bring you fish?" Archie asked her.

"Not *a* fish," Ava replied as she took another bite. "Usually about a hundred."

"Oh." Archie's head sank.

Not a quitter, he reminded himself. *Not a quitter.*

"But does Sonny tell you you have the most beautiful brown eyes he's ever seen?" he tried again. "Does he promise to fill your life with love and poetry and laughs?"

Ava sat back and thought for a moment. "No," she said a little sadly. "Mostly he just asks me when I think I'll be in heat."

"He sounds like quite a catch," Archie said, nodding.

Ava's dark face softened into a warm smile, and she laughed.

"Would you like to go for a walk, Archie?" she suddenly asked.

The bear frowned. "With you or alone?"

Ava chuckled again. "Come on," she said.

She led him along her favorite path, past the berry patch and through places more beautiful than any Archie had ever seen.

Along the way Archie stopped to pick wildflowers for Ava. And he couldn't resist showing her some of his most popular tricks.

After a while they came to the edge of the forest—a place where the huge trees gave way to a rocky cliff. They stopped and looked out over sparkling blue water stretching as far as they could see. And just when Archie thought he'd never find a more perfect view, his eyes landed on something that took his breath away. It was a beehive the size of a refrigerator, dangling out over the water like a gift from the honey gods.

"Wow!" he exclaimed, his eyes bulging at the sight. The tree it hung from could hardly hold it!

Ava nodded. "Bears have died trying to reach that hive," she told him.

Archie rolled back his shoulders and grinned proudly. "You want it," he told Ava, "it's yours."

"Don't even think about it," she said, waving the crazy idea away.

But he didn't seem to hear. "I'm going to get it for you," he announced with a bold step toward the bluff.

"Archie, I'm serious!" she cried, pulling him back. "Promise me you will never go up there! Promise me!"

He stepped back and turned toward her. "Okay." He shrugged. Then he grinned. "I like you, Ava," he said bashfully.

"I like you too, Archie."

She leaned over until her soft nose was almost touching his—when suddenly heavy footsteps *thud-thud-thudd*ed up behind them.

"What are you girls doing?" Sonny mumbled out of a honey-covered mouth. Bees were buzzing around his head, and his paws were dripping golden goo.

"Sonny, don't—" Ava began.

"Beat it, Circus Boy," the big grizzly told Archie, ignoring her completely.

"Sonny—"

"Keep your yap shut!" he snapped at Ava, whipping around.

"Ah, your charm is matched only by your odor," Archie said, stepping between the bully and Ava.

"What does that mean?" Sonny's heavy brow wrinkled.

"It means you're a malodorous ignoramus."

Sonny growled. "What is he saying?" the bear bellowed to Ava. "I'm confused! I don't like to be confused!"

Ava turned meekly to Archie and nodded. "He really doesn't."

"Really?" he said nonchalantly. "You'd think he'd get used to it."

"Let's go, Ava," Sonny grunted after one last snarl at Archie.

Then he ambled back into the forest. Sighing, Ava followed.

"Don't go!" Archie called after her. "Maybe you can do better than me . . . but don't do worse." He gazed after her miserably. "You like me, don't you?"

Ava turned and let a tear fall. "Of course I do, you fool," she told him. "But it can't work!" She looked at him sadly. "You'll always be a city bear."

Chapter 12

As the new day dawned, Archie awoke from a tortured sleep still racking his brain to figure out how he was going to get his girl, while outside the forest, in a greasy spoon in downtown Quincy, Dr. Dolittle was meeting with the other side.

"Shall we put all our cards on the table?" Mr. Potter asked him as the waitress set down three cups of lukewarm coffee.

Dolittle picked up his spoon and began to stir. "Of course."

The millionaire held up the front page of the *San Francisco Times*. In the center was a picture of Archie in his clown suit standing on a shiny bike.

"This bear you brought up here," Mr. Potter scoffed, "has as much chance of making little bear babies as Riley here." He nodded toward the grinning lawyer on his left. "Ain't a-gonna happen. On the other hand, thanks to you I'm not exactly drowning in favorable publicity." He frowned. "So here's my offer. I'll set aside ten acres—turn it into a sanctuary. You can move all your little animal buddies in there. Plus, you'll save face. You won't have to admit you failed and you won't look like a fool."

"Ten acres?" The doctor looked at him in disbelief. "That's ridiculous!" he said. Ten acres wouldn't sustain a petting zoo, let alone a whole forest's population.

"Dolittle, aren't you tired of looking like a schmuck?" Potter fired back. "You're an embarrassment to your profession. Oh, and how's your family enjoying their summer vacation?" Potter looked at him and smirked. "That's the offer. Take it or leave it."

Dr. Dolittle bit his lip. He wanted to say, "I'll leave it!" But the man had hit him where it hurt.

"The deadline is twelve noon next Wednesday." Jack Riley spoke up. "At twelve-oh-one, we're sending in every logger, every piece of logging equipment we've got. By Friday there won't be a tree standing."

The doctor looked from one man to the other. Then he let out a defeated sigh.

"Let me run it by my wife," he finally said.

"There's a pay phone in the back." Jack Riley grinned.

Reluctantly Dolittle pulled himself out of the

booth and walked to the back of the diner. He lifted the receiver from the pay phone and began to dial.

"*Psst!* Johnny!"

Dr. Dolittle turned and was stunned to see Archie peering in through a screen door.

"What are you doing here?" he asked.

The bear could hardly contain his excitement. "I came to tell you I'm in love!" he panted. "And Ava's in love with me!"

Dolittle's mouth fell open.

The sound of voices drifted toward them, bringing Dolittle to his senses again.

"Quick," said Dolittle, pushing open the men's room door. "Get in here!"

Archie followed the doctor into the cramped bathroom just as the cook came strolling by.

The doctor heaved a relieved sigh. Then he looked Archie in the eye.

"Look," he told the bear flat out, his face warmed by the bear's hot breath, "it's over. It's not your fault. It's mine. I started to believe my own press and bit off way more than I could chew. I'm sorry I dragged you into it."

He paused for a moment and sadly hung his head.

"Don't worry," he went on. "I'll get you an audition in Vegas or something. I've been offered a deal . . . and it's the best I can do."

"No!" Archie roared back. "The best you can do is not to give up on me."

The doctor stared at him, not sure at first that he was hearing the bear right. Was this the same Archie talking who had holed himself up in a tree?

"Doc," the bear continued, "you told me to listen to my inner bear. Well, I did. And I caught a fish!" He thumped his chest with his paw. "Me! Don't give up on me, Doc! Not now!"

"I don't know . . ." Dolittle shook his head.

"I know how I can win Ava!" Archie proclaimed.

The doctor eyed him, unconvinced. Then he slowly started to give in.

"All right," he finally said. "I've got to be nuts, but I'll give it one more chance."

"Yes!" Archie reached out to hug him. "Uh-oh," he grunted.

"What?" Dolittle asked.

Archie rubbed his bulging belly. "The ice cream's acting up."

"What ice cream?"

He hung his head. "I got depressed after Sonny and Ava went off together. I went on a bender back at the cabin. But by the second gallon," he confessed with a belch, "I realized I'm in love with a gal called Ava and an ice cream called Cherry Garcia. *Ohhh* . . ." He doubled over.

The doctor pulled as far away as he could. "Don't you be throwing up on me!" he said as he reached for the door.

Archie shook his head. "That's not where it's gonna come out," he said miserably.

"Oh, for—"

"I don't think I can hold it," the bear moaned.

"Then sit on the toilet," the doctor pleaded.

"The what?"

"The toilet!" Dolittle pointed to the porcelain commode behind him. "That thing!"

Archie collapsed on the covered seat. "Now what?" he groaned.

"You gotta lift the seat up!" Dolittle screeched.

He leaned over and yanked the seat up, and Archie looked down.

"Oh, I don't think that's gonna be big enough," he said. Then he doubled over once again. "Oh, boy . . ."

"Wait a minute!" the doctor shouted. He lunged for the door once more. "I'll be outside standing guard."

But when Dolittle opened the door, there was Jack Riley staring at him from the hall.

"Hi there," Dolittle said with a gulp, instantly jumping back. "Be right out. Just taking care of business."

The lawyer eyed him with suspicion. "Who are you talking to in there?"

"Oh . . ." The doctor shrugged nervously. "You know, sometimes you've got to coax it out. . . ." Then with a quick "Excuse me," he slammed the door in Riley's pasty face.

"Oh, no . . ." Archie was still moaning from the toilet.

"Wait, wait," Dolittle called out. "Don't start till I open a window!"

He reached for the bathroom's small window and fought to crack it open.

"Can't hold it!" the bear blurted out.

"No, no . . . ," Dolittle pleaded as he searched for something to throw through the glass.

But it was no use. The ice cream would not be deferred any longer. And Dolittle would not be spared its foul-smelling wrath.

Minutes later, Dr. Dolittle made his way back to the front of the diner—and at table after table, the people held their noses as he passed by.

At last he stopped in front of Potter and Riley and tried his best to look somewhat dignified.

"Gentlemen," he told them stiffly. "No deal. Thank you for your time."

Then, eyes tearing and gut wrenching, he staggered outside.

Chapter 13

While Dr. Dolittle was returning to the forest with Archie, his faithful daughter was back at the cabin, still struggling to follow in his footsteps.

"Can you hear me, Pepito?" Maya said as she sat eyeball to eyeball with the chameleon.

"Stop staring at me!" the lizard desperately tried to tell her. "You're freaking me out!"

But Maya just kept staring . . . and staring . . . and staring.

"What are you doing?" Charisse asked as she walked into the front room.

"I think he's about to say something," Maya replied, keeping her eyes glued to the scaly creature.

Charisse looked down at Pepito. "If he could

understand me," she said, crossing her arms, "I'd tell him how sick I am of all these stupid animals."

"Yeah," the chameleon shot back, "well, if you could understand me, I'd tell you to do something about those dandruff flakes. It's starting to look like Christmas in July."

Haughtily Charisse brushed past her sister and her pet and stomped out the back door.

"I hate this place!" she grumbled.

"And you're starting to get a butt on you, girl," the lizard called as he watched her go.

Outside Dr. Dolittle was just returning from town.

"Hey, honey," his wife called to him from the front porch swing. "How'd it go with Potter?"

The doctor climbed out of his Mustang and boldly slammed the door. "I told him no deal."

Lisa looked puzzled. "But I thought Archie wasn't working out."

"Well," replied the doctor, "he says he's got a plan to win Ava . . . so I'm going to see this thing through."

"You mean we're stuck here?" Charisse huffed. She balled her hands up into fists and angrily marched past her parents.

"Charisse!" Dr. Dolittle called, following her down the drive. He caught up with her and gently touched her on the shoulder.

"Hey . . . ," he began, "we're not getting along so good, are we?"

Charisse spun around. "I want to go home!" she cried as tears began to fill her eyes.

The doctor cradled her sad face in his hands. "I do too," he said. "And we will. But something else is going on with you, isn't it?" No matter how old his daughter got, he would always know when she was hurting.

Charisse looked down at her feet and silently watched a column of tears fall.

"Now, I'm not saying it's all your fault," her father went on. "I don't know what it is . . . if it's me or just your age or a phase one of us is going through . . . but . . ." He crossed his arms. "It's not pleasant."

Charisse sniffed. "I know," she whispered.

With his finger, Dolittle lifted her chin so that she looked at him. "Your mom thinks something's bothering you. Something you're not telling us."

Charisse blinked, looked away, and bit her lip. "No," she said after a beat.

"Because if there is," her father told her, "and I'm not saying there is—but if there is . . . we'd work it out. Like we always have. Right?"

"Right." His daughter nodded meekly.

"Okay?" he asked.

Slowly she nodded again.

Dolittle kissed her on the cheek and started back toward the cabin. "Dad . . . ," he heard her call.

"Yeah?" He spun around.

She opened her mouth—then seemed to change her mind.

"Nothing," she finally told him. She waved him toward the house. "Everything's fine."

And as she watched him walk away, she brushed a few white flakes from her shoulder.

Just after noon, Dr. Dolittle followed Archie to the site where he meant to win Ava back from Sonny.

"This is your big plan?" Dr. Dolittle asked with dread as he peered over the cliff.

"Yeah," Archie answered, with a determined nod. "If I can get the honey, it will prove I'm worthy of Ava."

"Yeah," said the doctor, "but if you fall, it'll prove you're stupid. And dead."

Archie shook off the comment, and with his eyes on the giant hive, he grabbed the tree and began to climb. "Wish me luck!"

"You come right back down here, young man," Dolittle called.

But Archie wouldn't stop. And within minutes word of his death-defying feat had spread throughout the forest.

"He's going after the hive!" the animals chattered.

Before long even Ava and Sonny had heard the word. And like everyone else, they hurried to see the crazy bear attempt to do what no bear had done before.

"I'm going to count to three and you better be down here!" Dolittle was still shouting.

But Archie had gone too far to turn back now. He was up the trunk and was starting to shinny out onto the narrow branch.

"Kid's got moxie," said the beaver. "I wish he had brains, too."

Finally Dr. Dolittle could stand it no more. He couldn't watch his friend just throw his young bear life away. A few more inches and the spindly branch was bound to break!

"Please don't do this," he begged Archie as he grabbed the trunk and began to climb up after him. "You're going to get hurt."

Archie patiently watched the doctor climb closer. "I don't think I'm going to win Ava by eating a bunch of worms," he tried to explain. "I'm never going to be more 'woodsy' than Sonny. I have to show her how much she means to me—*Uh-oh!*"

Suddenly Archie's hind paw slipped. He fought frantically to regain his hold. The branch dipped and bounced, heaving Archie around—and driving hundreds if not thousands of furious bees out of their hive! Instinctively they formed a noisy shield between the bear and the honey—and stayed there.

"Maybe I can talk to them—work something

out . . . ," Dolittle suggested. He gulped. "I've never talked to insects before."

He waved to the swarm and forced an innocent smile. "Hiya, boys. What's buzzin', cousin?"

"Sting, sting, sting, sting, sting, sting, sting . . . ," they simply replied.

"Can I speak to the queen?" Dr. Dolittle tried again.

"Sting, sting, sting, sting . . ."

"I'm dealing with very tiny minds," he observed unhappily.

Then all of a sudden—"*Attack!*" The command rang out from the hive and instantly the bees fell into formation. One by one, then all together, the bees rushed Archie and started to sting. But still they didn't stop Archie. He pulled himself along one more inch. Then, shielding his sensitive nose with one paw, he reached out the other . . . and grabbed the precious hive.

Unfortunately the huge bear's weight was too great for the branch. As Archie leaned out farther toward the end, the wood began to splinter and sag.

"Archie!" Ava gasped as the branch bent out of sight below the cliff. "Archieeee!"

"Bye-bye, Circus Boy," Sonny grunted beside her.

"Shut your fat face!" she growled.

The next thing the crowd knew, the branch sprang back up with Archie still clinging tightly to it.

It hadn't broken. Archie was okay—and he had the hive!

"Hooray!" the animals cheered.

Proudly, with the hive under one arm, Archie began to make his way back down the tree.

But it was too much for Sonny to take. As Archie's feet hit the ground, Sonny lunged for him, snarling and yelling, "Gimme that!"

The bully's teeth were bared and his fur was bristling. He was ready to do *anything* to get that hive away from Archie—and he probably would have if Archie hadn't stepped aside.

"*Ahhhhh!*" Sonny cried as he missed his target and tumbled over the rocky cliffside.

The animals waited a stunned moment . . . until a far-off splash told them Sonny had hit the water. Then Ava ran to Archie and the animals cheered once more.

"Hip-hip-hooray!"

"You did it, Doc," the raccoon beamed, running up to Dr. Dolittle.

"No, it wasn't me," replied the doctor with a modest shake of his head.

"Well, what then?" asked the possum.

Dolittle looked thoughtful for a moment. "What is it that makes you climb mountains, cross deserts, swim rivers . . . ?" he said.

"Usually a bigger animal chasing us," said the squirrel.

The doctor shook his head again. He turned his gaze on Ava and Archie, nuzzling next to the honey-filled hive.

"Love," he said simply. "Love."

Chapter 14

Finally, after what seemed like an endless celebration, the happy bear couple found themselves alone—just them and the giant hive.

"Honey?" Ava asked as she slowly licked her paw. She let the sweet nectar slide warmly down her throat. Then she closed her eyes and smiled.

"Yes, baby doll?" Archie replied, scooting closer to her.

"No," said Ava, giggling. "I meant would you like more honey?"

"Oh. No thanks . . ." Archie cleared his throat. "So, you ready to talk about where we go from here?"

Ava laughed again. "Talk is cheap," she teased. "Count to a hundred . . . and come get me!" And with a quick rub against Archie's nose, she bounded off into the forest.

Grinning, Archie leaned against an oak tree, closed his eyes and began to count.

"One . . . two . . . three . . . uh . . ." Archie frowned and rubbed his forehead. "One, two, three . . . uh . . ." Boy, that counting thing was tricky!

Oh well. He shrugged. "One! Two! Three! A hundred! Ready or not, here I come!"

Then all of a sudden—*crack!*—a shot rang out through the forest. And a long, pointed tranquilizer dart sank deep into Archie's rump.

"OW!" he cried out. "What the heck . . . ?"

But before he could finish his sentence, he was flat on his back, snoring.

As he fell, a shiny new pickup truck rumbled up from the fire road. On its side were painted the words POTTER INDUSTRIES. Quickly two men climbed out of the cab and dragged the bear into the truck. Then, as swiftly as they'd come, they jumped back in and drove off.

Moments later Ava trotted back into the clearing.

"Archie? Archie?" she called.

But it was too late. He was long gone.

Not much later, a tired but happy Dolittle was returning to his family, eager to spread the news that they had won.

"Daddy!" Maya shouted, jumping up from the porch steps. "Daddy's back!" she called to the cabin.

As his family came out, the doctor bounded up the path. But as he got closer he could tell that something wasn't right.

"What is it?" he asked.

Lisa hugged her arms close to her. "Archie," she replied.

As they sped into town, Lisa told Dolittle all she knew so far: Archie had been found plundering a local market, and Animal Control had been called in to stop him.

By the time the Dolittles arrived, police, forest service, and network news vehicles were lined up along Main Street.

The doctor had just parked outside the market when several Animal Control workers walked out with Archie on a stretcher.

The doctor ran up beside the unconscious bear. "What happened?" he demanded.

Another worker walked over and looked sadly from Dolittle to Archie.

"He broke down the back door," the man explained. "We found him ransacking the kitchen. Sorry, Dr. Dolittle," he said at last with a heavy sigh. "I was rooting for you."

Dolittle didn't see the man laugh and wink at Jack Riley as he walked away. He was too busy following Archie and the others to a waiting van.

As they lifted the bear in, Archie stirred and his eyelids fluttered open.

"Archie . . . Archie . . ." Dolittle leaned in. "It's me. What happened?"

The bear moaned and rolled his heavy head from side to side. "I don't know. I was meeting Ava at the oak tree. I was there. . . . Now I'm here."

Then his eyes drifted closed and he was asleep once again.

Lost and confused, Dolittle watched the men slide Archie's stretcher into the van and slam the doors after it. Then his eyes fell on Jack Riley talking to reporters in front of the store.

"We are setting aside ten acres, which we are calling the Dr. Dolittle Wildlife Sanctuary . . . ," he was saying as Dolittle stormed into view. "Why, speak of the devil." He grinned and waved.

"Let me tell you, Riley," Dr. Dolittle fumed, "you think you've won, but you haven't."

"Fine," the lawyer said, shrugging. "We'll level your forest and call it a tie."

But Dr. Dolittle wasn't going to lie down and roll over. Not now. Not ever!

———

Immediately Dolittle drove back to the forest—to the oak tree where Archie had said he remembered being last. He scoured the area, and it didn't take him long to find tire tracks and an empty tranquilizer bottle. It took him even less time to piece the story together in his mind and know in his heart that Potter was behind it.

But what good was the truth without witnesses to back it up? It was his word against Potter's—and that of everyone else on the old man's payroll. The doctor needed more proof. And he could think of only one guy who could help him. . . .

"If only we had an eyewitness," Dolittle sighed after he'd told the beaver his whole story. "Did anyone see anything?"

"Yeah . . . ," the beaver said, nodding. "Only problem is . . . he's a weasel."

"Why?" asked the doctor. "What did he do?"

"No." The beaver shook his head. "I mean he's an actual weasel."

He made a face, then waddled over to a nearby hole.

"Hey, weasel," he yelled down into the hole, "the doctor's here."

Moments later a beady-eyed weasel slinked out of the hole.

"That's *Mr.* Weasel," he said to the beaver, arching his long, silky back.

"Did you see what happened to the bear?" Dolittle asked eagerly.

"Maybe I did," the weasel replied. "Maybe I didn't."

Dr. Dolittle crossed his arms. "Did you see anything or not?"

The weasel coyly stroked his whiskers. "Sometimes I find my memory is jogged by a half dozen fresh eggs."

"You are such a weasel." Dolittle shook his head, disgusted.

"Thank you!" The creature smiled. "Now, about those eggs . . ."

Later that afternoon Dr. Dolittle went to Lisa to plan their legal strategy.

"It's simple," he told her as he paced the cabin floor. "Potter's guys set Archie up. I have a witness."

"An animal!" his wife exclaimed, trying to bring some sense back to the discussion. "You can't offer that as evidence."

"You got any other ideas?" he shot back.

"I can try and stall." Lisa sighed. "Get more time—maybe we can hire a private investigator."

"You're not going to get more time," Dolittle told

her. "Those trucks are ready to roll, and they're going to ship Archie out to a zoo in Mexico."

"John," she said, shaking her head at him sadly, "you go on the witness stand, Riley will tear you to shreds."

Dolittle held up his hands. "What do I have to lose?" he asked.

"Your reputation," she replied. "Your critics are going to have a field day with this one."

"I don't care," he said stubbornly. Archie was in lockup somewhere and the entire forest population was about to be tossed out on their furry behinds. "I can't give up on those animals without a fight."

Chapter 15

The day of the new trial, the courtroom was packed.

"I told you, Dr. Dolittle," the judge declared, "if that bear set paw in this town, your little experiment would be halted."

"Your Honor," Lisa said earnestly as she stood before the bench, "we admit the event was a setback, but we'd like another week to rehabilitate the bear."

Across the room Jack Riley rolled his eyes. "Perhaps counsel would like to check the animal into the Betty Ford Clinic," he joked. "Or is it the Yogi Bear Clinic?"

Lisa flashed him a warning look, then turned back to face the judge. "Then what if I could prove that the whole thing was a setup?" she asked.

The judge slipped off his glasses. "That's a very serious allegation," he replied, leaning forward attentively. "What proof do you have?"

Dr. Dolittle stood up beside his wife. "I have an eyewitness . . . ," he announced.

As the courtroom gasped, Jack Riley and Mr. Potter exchanged a nervous glance.

". . . who will testify," the doctor went on, "that he heard a gunshot and then heard a truck backing up to the area where the gunshot was heard."

"Is that witness here in the courtroom?" the judge asked.

"No, sir," Dolittle answered. "He's in the forest." He cleared his throat. "It's an animal."

Once again a sound traveled through the courtroom—only this time it was laughter.

"Order!" The judge banged his gavel and glared. "Dr. Dolittle," he grumbled, "did I hear you correctly? Your eyewitness is an *animal*?"

As his wife sank to her seat, the doctor nodded. "Yes, Your Honor," he replied. "A weasel."

"Ha! Ha! Ha!"

The courtroom exploded in laughter once more. And Riley and Potter's look changed to one of relief.

"Order!" the judge shouted.

"Your Honor," Dolittle pleaded, "I know this sounds unreasonable, but I can talk to the animals, and he did come forward with this information."

Jack Riley stood up. "Your Honor, I would not be opposed to allowing Dr. Dolittle or his counsel the opportunity to question this eyewitness. . . ." He grinned politely at the prosecution's table. "*But*—I would first like to go home and get my camera so I can take a picture of the animal being sworn in!"

As Riley chuckled at his own joke, giggles and comments again filled the air.

"That's enough!" the enraged judge barked.

"Does the weasel want immunity?" Riley went on, now playing to the amused crowd. "Should we put him in the animal protection program?"

Above the mayhem, the judge fumed—while Dolittle and his family's spirits sagged.

"Dr. Dolittle," the judge finally growled, "I will not allow you to make a mockery of my courtroom. The deadline has passed." He raised his heavy gavel. "Motion to extend denied."

Crrraaaack!

As the judge stormed out of the courtroom, the news media descended on Dolittle. For once, however, the doctor had no comment. Tight-lipped, he gathered his family and they fought their way out to their car.

After seeing Lisa and the girls back safely to the cabin, Dr. Dolittle took his Mustang and drove out to visit Archie.

The Animal Control guard showed him to a tiny cell where Archie lay with his back to the door, sighing heavily.

"Hey, Archie," the doctor called softly as the iron door clanged shut behind him.

Archie lifted his head, then jumped up in front of Dolittle, excited.

"Doc!" he exclaimed. "What happened? Are they going to let me out?"

"Well . . ." Dolittle gulped. "Sort of."

"Sort of?" Archie looked puzzled.

"I couldn't prove your story," the doctor explained. "They . . ." His pained voice trailed off.

"They what?"

Dolittle laid his hand on Archie's shoulder. "They won't let you go back to the woods," he said. "They say you're too dangerous. So they . . ." Once again the words got caught in his throat.

"Yeah?" Archie prodded.

". . . sold you to a Mexican circus." Dr. Dolittle choked back a sob.

"*Ay, chihuahua.*" Archie slumped down onto his rump and let his head fall to his paws.

"Archie, I'm sorry, man." Dolittle sadly shook his head.

"For what?" Archie sighed.

"For everything—dragging you out here, putting

you through everything, giving you hope. I ruined your life."

"Ruined my life?" The bear raised his shaggy head and looked into Dolittle's eyes. "Doc, you *gave* me a life! You're the one who taught me about love. To be a bear among bears. No one can ever take that away from me."

Touched, the doctor choked back another sob and sank down beside his furry friend.

Just then the cell door clanked open and a guard let Charisse in.

"Charisse!" Dolittle exclaimed.

"Mom sent me in to tell you that her motion for an appeal has been denied," she told him with a pained expression.

"Oh." Dolittle sighed. "Well, we knew it was a long shot. . . ."

He gave Charisse a halfhearted smile and watched her head toward the door. Then he turned his attention back to Archie.

"Look," he told the bear, trying to focus on the bright side, "at least you'll be back in show business."

"It's not what I want anymore," Archie replied. "I want Ava."

"I know." The doctor nodded.

Archie gazed longingly at the photo of Ava he'd

taped to his concrete wall. "Maybe I wasn't *meant* to be loved," he sniffed.

"Everybody's meant to be loved."

Startled, both Archie and Dolittle looked up to see Charisse still standing by the door. Had she just responded to what Archie had said?

"How did she know what I said?" Archie turned to the doctor.

"She— You— How—?" Dr. Dolittle was speechless. "Oh my God," he finally gulped. Charisse could communicate with animals too!

Chin trembling and eyes rimmed with red, his daughter nodded.

"Since when?" he asked her.

"A few weeks," she confessed. "First it was just kind of . . . fuzzy and vague. Only now . . ." She bit her lip. "It's real clear."

"Is that what you were keeping from us?" Dolittle guessed.

Charisse nodded and wrung her hands, and finally let her tears begin to fall.

"I didn't want to admit it," she sobbed as she moved into her father's arms, "because I didn't want to be a freak."

"Honey." Dolittle gently stroked her hair. "I'm sorry. I know what it feels like. When it happened to me, I went crazy. But you're looking at it wrong." He leaned back and touched her cheek. "It's a *good* thing."

Charisse looked doubtful. "Yeah?"

"Sure." Her father nodded. "Hey, look at the good it's done already."

Charisse frowned. "What good?"

"Well, look at *us*!" The doctor smiled and wrapped her in his arms once more.

"Boo-hoo-hoo!"

Dolittle and Charisse looked over to see their bear friend blubbering in a sea of tears.

"It's just so beautiful," he wept between bawls and sloppy sniffles. "A father and daughter happy together . . . just one of the things I'll never have."

"Daddy." Charisse turned to her father. "We have to help him. Isn't there something we can do?"

Dolittle shrugged helplessly.

"It's not just him, Dad," Charisse went on. "It's *all* the animals. I mean, there are so many of them."

"Yeah," Dolittle agreed. "There are . . ." Suddenly his eyes lit up. ". . . so many of them!"

Chapter 16

That night, with a plan freshly brewing in his mind, Dr. Dolittle returned to Campbell's Grove.

He was alarmed to find that the clear-cutting had just about begun—and that the animals were packed and preparing to go. How could they just run away?

"You guys have given up, haven't you?" he asked them.

Bitterly they looked away.

"Even you?" He stared at the beaver. "You're giving up?"

"What am I gonna do?" the beaver sulked. "I'm six years old. I'm not a young man. Besides, we've been living in this forest how long now?" He looked up at a tree full of birds.

"My family tree goes back about one point six million years," a raven replied.

"So we had a good run," the beaver said, shrugging.

"All the more reason not to give up," Dolittle told him. "Look, I thought I could do this alone, but I can't. If you want to save your homes, you've got to help me." He gazed at all the downcast faces surrounding him. "Because you have enormous untapped power."

The raccoon grumbled. "Yeah, but you got the thumbs."

Dr. Dolittle shook his head. "I don't—"

"It's the only reason you're there and we're here," the raccoon went on. "You got the thumbs."

"Yeah," rumbled the other animals. "That's right. That sucks."

"Okay, okay." Dr. Dolittle held up his hands to quiet them down. "Maybe we do have thumbs, but you got something we don't have." He grinned and pumped his fists like a cheerleader. "Strength. Courage. Perseverance."

"Oh, come on . . . ," the animals groaned. "Get real. . . ."

"It's true!" declared the doctor. "When people talk about the best of the best, it's always an animal expression. 'The heart of a lion.' 'The strength of an ox.' 'The grace of a gazelle.' 'Sly as a fox.' 'Smells like a skunk.'"

"Hey!" the skunk shouted.

"Sorry." Dolittle's face grew earnest and solemn. "Listen. Together, I swear you can do it. Don't give up without a fight."

Two by two, all eyes turned toward the wise old beaver.

"Get out the word," he said at last with a decided flap of his tail. "As of today . . . the trucks don't move!"

"Hooraaaay!"

The next morning Campbell's Grove was filled with trucks, bulldozers, and chain saws raring to go. But it was also filled with creatures ready to risk their lives to stop them.

As the sun lit up the sky, Charisse, Maya, and Eric pedaled up on shiny bikes.

"Hey, kids," a burly logger called as they plopped down in front of a tree. "I'm going to have to ask you to move."

Charisse looked up at him and squared her shoulders. "No," she said.

The burly man shifted his saw. "Listen, kids, don't start with us—"

"All right, everybody," Charisse suddenly barked in animal tongue. "Take your places."

And like a flash, a pack of wolves appeared from behind the trees to form an animal barrier in front of the machines.

"That's right," Eric told the dumbstruck logger. "My girlfriend's got the talk-to-animals mojo! Didn't see that coming, didja?"

"Strike! Strike! Strike!"

Throughout the forest, and for as far as word could travel, animals everywhere joined in the common chant of nonviolent, nonhuman protest.

"Strike! Strike! Strike!"

On dairy farms cows refused to give milk.

Chickens refused to lay eggs.

Dogs refused to walk.

Cats refused to use their litter boxes.

"It's ridiculous," Mr. Potter growled as he clicked on the TV. His crooked face was red and twitching. "Animals can't *organize*!"

"Take a look for yourself," Jack Riley told him, nodding toward the latest news.

"All over the world, animals have organized," a reporter announced. *"Paris . . ."*

On the screen flashed a scene of monkeys loose in a French park, tossing food and singing bawdy socialist anthems.

". . . Australia . . ."

Crocodiles marched in the streets.

". . . and Brooklyn . . ."

Even turtles were picketing along the Brooklyn Bridge.

Potter's fleshy jowls dropped.

"Maybe you should call Dolittle," Riley told him.

"And what?" snapped the millionaire. "Give in to a bunch of beasts and lower life-forms? I've taken on the Democrats, I can take on a bunch of animals."

Just then ten or twenty squealing rats dashed across the floor toward him.

Unfazed, Potter raised his foot and stomped it loudly on the rug.

"Organize, my foot," he snarled.

Then, grabbing his coat, he marched out of his office. If he had to chop down every one of those trees in Campbell's Grove himself, he would.

With his lawyer scurrying behind him, Potter stormed out of his office building into the parking lot.

"Beat it!" he yelled to a raven perched beside the exit.

He was continuing toward his car when, from above, a commanding-looking bird began squawking. Suddenly a flock of birds dive-bombed Potter and Riley, covering them with milky bird poop.

"Ahhhh!" Potter cried as Riley tried to shield himself from the deluge. They were under attack!

But when the pair turned around to flee to the office, they discovered a growling wolf blocking their way.

"Nice doggie," Riley said, his voice trembling.

Slowly Potter and Riley turned again and hurried down another path . . . only to find themselves face to face with a swarm of angry bees.

The men dropped their briefcases and began to run. They made a dash for the office building, with Potter steps ahead of a hysterical Jack Riley.

The millionaire yanked the door open and ran inside, letting the steel door slam shut behind him. Seconds later Riley ran up and pulled on the door . . . only to find that it was locked.

Desperate, he pounded on the door. "Mr. Potter!" he cried. "Let me in!"

But his boss didn't seem to hear him.

Trembling, Riley turned around to face the buzzing bees. "I just work for him!" he pleaded. "I was on your side from the very beginning! *Aaaahhhhh!*"

Safe inside his office, Potter leaned against the door and sighed.

"Oh, well," he chuckled as he listened to the muffled screams coming from outside. "Guess I've gotta get myself another lawyer."

Then he stood up and laid his hand on a stuffed bear, one of his many hunting trophies.

"You're the guy that locked up my boyfriend," the stuffed bear growled.

"*AHHH!*" Potter jumped. The furious bear was alive!

"P-p-please, don't," he stammered. "Please, I'm sure we can work something out."

He staggered backward and into another trophy— a fat raccoon—only to find that it was real too.

As Potter stood there shaking, Ava and Joey moved in closer, growling and snarling and generally making his heart race.

"Okay, okay," he said at last, reaching into his pocket. "I'm just getting my phone, see? I'm calling Dr. Dolittle, okay?"

With a grin, Ava looked at the raccoon and waited. . . .

Brrinnggg! Brrinngggg!

Out at the cabin, Dr. Dolittle got up from the dinner table and picked up the telephone.

"Ah, Mr. Potter . . . Call what off?" He grinned at his family. "You don't actually think animals can organize, do you, Mr. Potter?"

"I—I don't know *what* to think anymore," Potter stammered over the phone. All he knew for sure was that a big, angry bear had him backed into a corner.

"Shall we put our cards on the table?" Dolittle mockingly suggested. "I'm willing to set up a meeting between you and the animals to work it out."

"What!"

"That way you'll save face. You won't have to admit you failed and you won't look like a fool."

Mr. Potter frowned. Then he felt Ava's moist drool streaming hotly down his neck.

"Anything," the old man gasped. "Please. Just, for the love of God, call them off."

Dr. Dolittle covered the receiver and laughed.

"Okay," he said when he'd recovered. "Let me talk to the raccoon."

Obediently Potter handed the phone over.

"Oh, come on," Joey pleaded, "just an arm or something?" He rolled his eyes and grumbled. "Oh, fine."

He dropped the phone and nodded up at Ava. "We're outta here!" he told her.

And as the two ambled out the door, Potter collapsed in a sweaty heap. "Thank God!"

Chapter 17

The Potter/Animal Summit took place as prom-
ised first thing the next day.

"I just want to say that I am here as a mediator
only," Dr. Dolittle told the anxious parties gathered
around the conference table. On one side sat Potter
and a swollen-faced Jack Riley. On the other side
were the beaver, the raccoon, the possum, and the
weasel.

"These negotiations will be between you, Mr.
Potter," Dolittle explained, "and the representatives
of the United Forest Animals Local 534."

Mr. Potter leaned over the donuts and animal
chow and handed Dolittle a sheet of paper. "This is
my new proposal," he said.

The doctor took it and began to read.

"Twelve acres!" he exclaimed, shaking his head in disbelief.

Potter nodded proudly, impressed with his own bold and selfless generosity.

"Grab him," the beaver muttered. "I'm gonna eat him!"

Murmurs of agreement rumbled around the table.

"They like it, I can tell." Potter beamed at the doctor.

Then he watched the possum climb onto the table and squat over the document.

Dolittle looked from the soaked paper to the slackjawed man.

"That would be a *no*," he told Potter.

Twenty-four hours later Dr. Dolittle presented Potter with the fifteenth draft of the forest animals' proposal.

"Do we have a deal?" he asked wearily as the businessman read.

Mr. Potter frowned. It was clear he still didn't like it. And without saying a word, he stood up and reached for his fly.

"Mr. Potter!" the doctor cried.

The millionaire crossed his arms. "Oh, but it's fine when *they* do it!" he grumbled.

Then with a sigh he sat back down and held out his stubby hand. "Just hand me a pen," he huffed.

And with a flick of his wrist, the deal was done.

While Potter Industries saw that the trucks and bulldozers were removed from Campbell's Grove, Dr. Dolittle and his family saw that Archie was released from Animal Control and returned to his new home . . . and future wife.

For the doctor it was another job well done. And better yet, he and Charisse were closer than ever before, now that she too could talk to animals. Charisse had even taken over helping Pepito with his colors . . . or at least she'd redone her room in bright green so he'd feel like he was blending in.

But the best news of all came early the next spring, when out of Archie and Ava's hibernation hole crawled two tiny Pacific Western bear cubs.

"No, no, no," Archie instructed his cubs patiently as Ava watched, smiling. "Stop wrestling with your sister and focus!" he was telling them. "It's step, step, *turn*, kick, step."

"Papa, I thought it was step, *kick*, turn, step, step," one of the cubs complained, hopping around on the rocks.

Yes, thanks to Dr. Dolittle there were two brand-new Pacific Western bears in Campbell's Grove, ready to take on the world . . . and, if Archie had anything to do with it, ready to open in six weeks.